To my lo[...]
Please en[...]
first book ☺ Pass it on and keep returning it to small roadside libraries.

# Starting Again

Thank you for your support
Keep supporting local businesses
Proudly Canadian
Nathalie Edwards

# Nathalie Edwards

www.nathalieedwards011.com

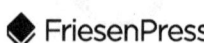
FriesenPress

One Printers Way
Altona, MB R0G 0B0
Canada

www.friesenpress.com

**Copyright © 2025 by Nathalie Edwards**
First Edition — 2025

All rights reserved.

No part of this publication may be reproduced in any form, or by any means, electronic or mechanical, including photocopying, recording, or any information browsing, storage, or retrieval system, without permission in writing from FriesenPress.

Chapter header graphics by Vecteezy.com

ISBN
978-1-03-833160-1 (Hardcover)
978-1-03-833159-5 (Paperback)
978-1-03-833161-8 (eBook)

1. FICTION, ROMANCE, CONTEMPORARY

Distributed to the trade by The Ingram Book Company

Dedication
In the least narcissistic way, this book is dedicated to me. I have overcome some fierce challenges over my lifetime, especially in the last couple of years. This allowed me the time and space to accomplish something I have always wanted since I was little. This book is proof that with belief in one's self, and perseverance, we can all tap into potential that is in abundance within. We can accomplish goals and simply be epic.

Thank You
With that said, there are many people I would like to thank. I am lucky to have so many wonderful people in my life who have supported me, encouraged me, and accepted me in all my weirdness. To all my family and friends, thank you. A special thank-you to my husband Darren and son Davven, and to Vicky who helped me at the very start.

# Introduction
## Charlie Wolfe

And so, as history will be written, it became that in 2020 having cancer had been a blessing and we were all thankful that cancer was not discriminating.

Two very odd things to say about cancer, but as fate would have it, cancer saved about eighteen million people. How, you ask? Well, in 2019 the world faced a pandemic of a new virus. It spread quickly, killed mercilessly, and it split the world into two groups. Those who believed in the pandemic and a vaccine, and those who didn't on both counts.

It took about a year and a bit for a vaccine to be whipped up and manufactured, three distinct brands rushed to the rescue as fast as they could. In the meantime, countries closed their borders to travel, where others had forced quarantine. A variety of in-between for each country, province, state, and city.

The world went into an epic panic, and to be honest, why wouldn't they. No one was prepared, there were no answers except for the healthy measures of "stay away from each other" or "stay home if you are sick." Warnings issued for all of us to be prepared to spend at least two weeks isolated in our homes. In moments of panic, we as humans sometimes thrive or lack luster. In that moment we lacked luster, raiding stores for food and household items, stockpiling cleansing wipes, toilet paper, and NyQuil that we would never use entirely, rubbing alcohol flew off shelves.

I remember grocery stores being cleaned out of products and produce, rows of empty shelves. Stores had to start putting a limit on items to ensure everyone got a little of everything. For me, personally, it was an issue when the liquor stores started doing that. Take the toilet paper, the NyQuil, and the beef, but leave me my wine.

I had a drinking problem by this point, which had led to my liver cancer diagnosis and subsequently a fight for my life. Where your sentence was bleak or hopeful, with cancer you always face your mortality. Cancer in itself is the scariest word and diseases known to man. But my drinking problem was not a result of the pandemic as many had joked would happen. I have had a drinking problem since my twenties, so twenty years when the pandemic swept over all the earth's inhabitants.

So, why was cancer a blessing and we were all grateful for the fact that it wasn't discriminating against age, sex, gender, or what you did for a living? A series of events that you would not have strung together in normal times, to have any impact on each other, just happened to during 2020 when the vaccines started to hit the market.

By chance, as I hear it, it all started with a cancer patient on their deathbed wishing to stop treatment and travel; to see a part of the world before they died, needed a vaccine and was administered one before they could travel. Vaccines were mandatory for travel between 2020 and 2022, once the first and second and millionth wave of mutated strands hit.

## *Starting Again*

A wonderful story that ended up being a lonely person, living out their last months, riding the tails of the effects of the previous chemo treatments, vaccinated to travel. Boarding a plane thinking *this is it, my last trip. I am going to such and such to live out my last days on a beach or terrace* and wouldn't you know it, to their surprise and of those who found out about the story, that the vaccine had actually cured them.

In medicine for dummies terms, the vaccine bullied out the cancer in its effort to inject a mild-dose of the virus to help build antibodies. It built antibodies, all right. Big angry ones that had a taste for cancer cells and went to work. If you didn't believe in miracles, this would come close to impressing you. After months of living abroad, and instead of feeling worse every day, this person started to feel better and outliving the expected two to three months.

Word spread quickly, tests were made, vaccines administered. Not enough nurses on the planet to administer the vaccine in the speed in which it was in demand. It was the miracle cure humanity had been working on for the last three decades. Poof, just like that, a happy series of events.

And here I and millions of other cancer survivors stand. The last of humanity as it turns out on earth. I was at the end, like so many others, and this savior in the form of a needle and the symbolic nurse flicking the bubbles out of the syringe. And not only those in hospital with a diagnosis, but those also living with cancer and not knowing. People who just didn't feel right, an ache here or pain there, joyfully felt relief after getting the vaccine.

Well, I can tell you that the campaign ads to get the vaccine wrote themselves after this discovery. People clamoring for their turn, pushing Grandma out of the way with no remorse. Unfortunately, and perhaps because it was rushed a little due to the circumstances, the vaccines did not have such a positive effect on the rest of the populous. The virus worked fast, killed swiftly, and the vaccines were no match. I think everyone was so focused on the miracle of curing cancer that everyone else was lost in the cracks. By the time there was enough data to say that it wasn't working, it really wasn't working. Billions lost their lives and we all lost someone.

A pandemic doesn't enter the lives of humans without leaving a scar one way or another. Despite being so grateful, grateful beyond words to be alive, I live with survivors' guilt and grieve the loss of my friends and family. I thankfully didn't have any children and never married; hard to maintain relationships with people when I had a very toxic one already with alcohol. I couldn't even imagine burying your children or spouse.

Here we are now in 2024, just about eighteen million survivors trying to make sense of it all, work through our crap and rebuild society. This is where the non-discriminatory part really comes into focus: while we are trying to rebuild, those of us still around don't have to reinvent the wheel. Doctors get cancer, engineers get cancer, the young and old, black and white, they all got cancer. We didn't have to go back to *Little House on the Prairie*'s time, we just had to reimagine what life looked like before.

It was very much like end of times; Stephen-King-apocalyptic clearing streets and homes and cars of the dead. It wasn't a clean fadeout to stage left; people died everywhere. Waiting for a miracle of their own, trying to make sense of what I am sure they knew could be the end of their precious time here on earth.

Organically over time, everyone just did their part and then started living the life they wanted. Unapologetic but very harmoniously with each other and with the environment. It was Mother Nature's hidden agenda in the pandemic and her stance on the outcome. We had ruined her earth, and she fixed the problem in one fell swoop. Not with tsunamis or flash freezing, but with a virus that takes out the parasites doing the damage.

## *Starting Again*

Her vision also was clear when putting cancer with the vaccine, and having a new group of humans now immune to a very deadly disease. But reportedly approximately eighty percent of survivors cannot procreate, we have been rendered sterile. A gift wrapped in a slap in the face. Curing us only to let our species die out over time. Again, weirdly enough, we are grateful that cancer isn't discriminating, allowing for babies to toddlers to children of all ages needing parents. Leaving the need for adoption of those orphaned who were cured of their cancer at young ages.

As for me, being an alcoholic and cancer survivor, I want a life without chaos. Quietness, stillness. Being drunk all the time causes this unconscious noise and chaotic TV series on repeat in your mind. And the longer you are an alcoholic, the more you get used to the chaos, and even start being dependent on it as part of your identity.

Which brings me to my story, where I found peace and joy and happiness. With no ties to my home in the United States, I moved to the most beautiful place on earth, Vancouver Island, British Columbia, Canada.

# Introduction

## Everett Peterson

Like every other living human right now in 2024, I am only here because cancer saved my life. The last five years have been unbelievable, and no one would or will believe it unless you were there. Losing almost every human being on the planet to a virus and those who remain, survived because they were dying of a disease when the pandemic started.

Silver lining, I guess, is that we now have a cure for cancer, which only cost us the lives of billions of people. But Mother Nature had said it was so and we are only tenants on her land so that is how the history books will be written.

After all the radiation and chemo fried my hair, five years later it was nice to have my thick brown hair back. I have not cut it since it started to grow back. For me my hair is a symbol of my healing, but I'll cut it one day. Just not today. Brain cancer almost got me, but my hair is a symbol of a big fuck you and I like that. And since I'm giving cancer the big F-U, I let the beard grow in, too.

Most survivors have now moved to bigger cities, those naturally just had more people to start with, and stores and necessities at hand. And if not in the city, not too far. We lost so many lives, and that includes animals that were trapped in a house or car. Farm animals did all right for those that were able to roam free or had access to some sort of food and water.

With all the death and clean-up taken care of, there is still grief and guilt and heartbreak. But we all have a bit of relief with the newfound quietness and we don't have to deal with dead bodies. Being with the Canadian Navy, anyone with that kind of background aligned with the military to help remove the bodies and dispose of them. Having rotting humans all over the world was bad for everyone. They needed to be removed from water systems and out of reach of scavengers.

I didn't mind so much, had thick skin already from death being part of my livelihood for years, or maybe I just push down, store it away, and try to forget the faces of all the dead bodies. And like I said, it is quiet now, humanity seems to have settled down a bit, taking a knee and taking a minute to reflect. No fighting or big declarations of who's dick was bigger. Those who survived have seemed to prioritize correctly what was actually important, to live a full and happy life and to just let your neighbors do the same.

Knowing we all have a similar appreciation for life having survived cancer, knowing none of us have the will or want to put energy into being an asshole, has left the space for peace and general contentment. We are all minorities now. I remember a comedian once saying that the answer to racism was to just mix everyone with everyone, well, we didn't have the fun of mixing everyone with everyone, but this also presented as a solution. Eventually there won't be any distinctive ethnicities.

Like most, I am just trying to figure out my place in this new world. I have no family left, I had no children of my own or wife, and all my immediate family has passed. I am grateful to have been there for them in the end like they had planned and tried to do for me when I thought my end was coming. I am grateful that we were all at home: my mother, my father, my brother, and nephew. At the beginning of the pandemic they encouraged creating bubbles of people you wanted to live with because of the quarantine, so that is just what we did. We had already done that anyway; with cancer you can't have people bringing in colds or flus or infections.

I watched each of my loved ones take their last breath, holding a hand or stroking their hair and waiting until they all passed before releasing all the sadness welling and festering in my chest. These memories I will shove way down and store away with all the other memories I choose not to deal with.

Off to find my little slice of heaven. Don't want a big city but can't stay here. Too many memories and the town is small with little nearby. Feeling pretty great about surviving cancer and this pandemic, but a man needs to eat and still find safety in numbers. I'm going to move down island to Victoria and see if anything speaks to me.

How you might be wondering, what about money? Well, believe it or not, with so few people and so much actual currency, we just sort of all decided to deal with that later since it lost so much value. But everything was there for the taking to start over. You could take what wasn't already someone else's, and with so few people, pretty much everything you could find in a store, in a house, or on the road was free.

# Chapter 1

# Charlie

Despite life mostly staying somewhat normal, travel did take a hit. And not that it isn't possible, but it is much different and requires way more patience. On the upside, border travel is just as easy as take one step after another, there is no border patrol or security. Good or bad, it made my travel experience better.

*Why am I leaving*? I asked myself a few times in the last month or so. The pandemic is over, this place is familiar, why leave? I asked myself aloud a few times, "Why do I want to leave, why not stay?" And to be honest the answer is this place just had too many memories of loss. Yes, surviving cancer is in the gain column, but the loss of my parents and brother was and is just too much. Seeing neighbors' and friends' dead bodies being carried out of their homes, their cars, in the street, or at stores during what I called the clean-up still haunted me.

The main reason that I had to leave was because I was an alcoholic before getting cancer. Quitting wasn't my choice, it was forced on me. Don't get me wrong, it saved my life, the forced choice, but still wasn't mine. Again, yes, it had to be done, but with it not being my choice I haven't really grieved the loss of who I was, haven't really accepted this is me now.

I was trashed one minute and the next getting chemotherapy and told drinking wasn't an option so to consider myself in recovery. I have no idea who I am or what I'm capable of. I have no idea what I like and don't like doing now that I'm sober. I have been sober for two years now, but this is the first time that really I have the space to ask those questions. I got sick, went into treatment, thought I would die, came to terms with that, the scare of a pandemic, thought I would die from that, a cure (YAY), but everyone else died (BOO). Then there was the aftermath and chaos of, *what the fuck do we do now?*

I have started reminding myself daily of what I'm grateful for, and most of the time I am grateful that I am sober and alive to be there for my family in their last moments. I'm also grateful for the gift of going to bed sober and not pass-out drunk. I am slowly learning that gratitude is the key to staying positive. But I have to be honest, I would kill for a drink. And still wanting to drink on a daily basis instills such rage in my body, I can't get over that I still feel that way. I am learning it will never go away.

All I can think to do is find somewhere quiet, in the mountains, because I love mountain views with a lake, start a farm and live off my land. With so much land now available (which still makes me feel icky inside to think that we are just free willy taking something that used to belong to someone else) and with no one to buy it from you can stake claim on a plot of land, becoming the new owner and whatever you find on it.

So the question of the hour is: Where to go to find my own oasis? I have always wanted to go to British Columbia, Canada.

Seattle is just a stone's throw. It took me two days to make the decision and get shit in motion. And here we are now, on Vancouver Island, ready for the next chapter.

Now is a beautiful, crisp morning in May. The sun is shining ridiculously happy rays for seven a.m. The sun isn't warm but it is warming my soul; making this decision feels right. The cool air teasing the exposed skin on my hands and face. This felt good and for the first time my rage is temporarily tampered down with a feeling I hadn't felt truly for a long time: just pure happiness.

I traveled by car, stopping when I could for gas, there aren't many stations and even if you did find one no guarantees it was functional. So I switched cars a few times, too, when they ran out of fuel. But the biggest challenge was timing for the ferry once I had crossed over to Vancouver. The trick to getting to the island is there are no bridges. But Vancouver Island calls to me, it is more isolated, yes, but I wanted to be alone to a certain extent. And an island with no bridges seemed simply perfect.

God, BC is beautiful with the Rockies and the ocean views. The temperatures here were very agreeable. Flowers in bloom and the grass is already green. Crossing the big vastness of the ocean is almost therapeutic. Looking into the depths of the water you get lost, and it feels like someone is reading your soul.

Days went by and I never talked to a soul. One of the only times was on the ferry. It was nice to see those who continued with certain jobs or tasks that you might think everyone would have abandoned, like driving the ferry or running a gas station. Money had lost most of its value and we still sometimes pay for the services, but in times like these where everyone is doing what they want to do and not what they have to, payment is usually a thank-you. It is sadly surprising that some of these dreadfully mundane activities, someone still genuinely loved doing them.

I took a few days to drive around the island to see if anywhere spoke to me. I took up journaling and meditating to pass the time and get over my anger. I was a bit lonely and sometimes the sheer lack of people made me feel claustrophobic strangely enough. The vastness felt and still feels like a big coffin.

I had a vision in mind, of what my new life would be. Back in Seattle I worked an office job, but deep down my creative side was dying. It sucked the soul out of my eyes with the repetition and the knowledge that if I died one day I would be replaced without hesitation. I didn't feel like I mattered.

My new life had life in it: animals and gardens and in the effort to appease Mother Nature, it would all be eco-friendly. My vision would be eco-friendly and self-sustaining. I would turn into a hippie hermit. Sitting in my car having a snack on the side of Highway 1, my hippie hermit thought made me smile and turn my head to look out the window. This large, beautiful valley lay just a few feet away. A farmhouse and barns nestled in the center. In the back surrounding it all is a spectacular mountain range with the peaks covered in snow. Close to my vision, but nothing spoke to me or drew me close.

So my travels continued, and the journey is not only physical in the sense of looking for a home, but the other type of journey, the one I am on with discovering me and what I could really accomplish.

# Chapter 2

## Charlie

**Journal entry**
May 2, 2024

"People don't connect like they used to. It is quiet to a different level of profound, when you are outside your home. Well, for me anyway. I saw the most beautiful valley along the highway, deep rich evergreens lining the edge of the floor all the way up to the mountains that surrounded the valley. Snow peaks to contrast the vibrant green, and I caught it at sunrise so streams of peach highlighted the tips of the highest treetops. In the valley was a working farm, I could see life of people. The people looked like little Lego people moving around bustling, feeding animals, and doing other farm stuff. I want that, I have never done that, but I want that. Life is so strange without my bad habit. I am coming to terms with that loss; I actually think I prefer myself and my life this way. I have no idea if being cured means I can't get cancer again, but I don't hate myself enough to try. I think I actually like myself. So much has happened, and I don't know or think I will ever be able to process it all, but deep down in my bones I know that I want a home that brings me inner peace, self-worth, and happiness. I don't think I have ever truly felt happiness, well, until I stopped for a few minutes to gaze upon that valley. I am scared and I don't know why being sober scares me. Maybe because I don't know who I am yet or I have forgotten how to cope without being drunk. I just want for one day that I don't think of drinking at any point. I think moving is just a way to move away from who I was. Start new and fresh with a new me. I miss my family, we had our ups and downs, mostly because of my drinking, but they always wanted this for me, to be sober and they meant well. Strange to have a phone but no one to text or call. Oh, and happy birthday to me."

And with that, I put pen and journal away and start making my way down to Victoria, BC, in search of my mountain views with a lake. The day is clear and the sky even clearer. Since the pandemic with less air travel, the blueness of the sky is brighter and untainted by jet streams. I stopped at a beach access along the way a couple of days ago and there was no telling where the ocean ended and the sky started, blue as can be. I felt soothed and grounded just being near the ocean. Mesmerized by waves slowly rolling in and gently crashing into the shore. Barely a sound, all you could hear were seagulls and sea lions. The sky was the same color as that day and from the warmth of my car it just felt like summer.

I passed an old provincial park area called Goldstream and took the first exit off the highway after that. Looked beautiful, with big rainforest trees covered in the lime-greenest moss you have ever seen. All over the branches, hanging in the sunshine, almost looking like transparent sunbathers. I'll have to go back but for now will explore this area for the day.

The strangest thing, for a woman, is to feel safe traveling and exploring alone. Not only are there fewer people but violence and

## Starting Again

crime doesn't seem worth anyone's time anymore. We all have equal opportunity to start new and create whatever we desire. You want to farm? Go ahead. You want to build Lego all day and night? No one can stop you. You want to be a photographer? You can make a living off that without being any good.

I feel safe sleeping in my car or anywhere. Worst predator these days, I guess, here on the island are wolves. Or a bear, but they don't eat you. Feeling safe shares a place with feeling overwhelmed with the deafening silence. Both are very unnerving sometimes, but very pleasant in the same breath.

I've turned down this little dirt road, didn't see the name, but it looked promising, if not only for an adventure. And I couldn't believe my eyes when I rounded a turn and the space opened up to show off a big old property. It looked fully fenced with signs of animals. The house looked in good order from the road so I thought I would make my way up and see. I stopped just at the end of the driveway and took it all in.

Behind the house is the most gorgeous mountain view I have ever seen; clean and crisp details. I could see the snow peaks, rock formations peeking out of the forests of evergreens that drizzled down the side getting thicker and thicker towards the bottom. All around, a true 360-degree view. Looking closer, instead of up and away, I can see fields of green grass, contrasted by fields of hay. A farm-style wood fence as far as I could see.

A gravel road leading up a slight incline to a house, a white house, and behind it a worn red barn. Nothing giant, nor run-down looking. Seems to have held up well. I'll have to see about electricity and running water. Both are still functioning as normal in most places, the only difference is we as a society now don't pay for any of it. For the time being. Stores are not manned but still function with electricity so most frozen or canned food didn't go bad. Unfortunately, with no stockpile or delivery service, once they were out they were out.

I grabbed as much as I could as I found it, grabbed stuff like veggies seeds, too, just in case. Most inhabited homes had gardens nowadays, it is the only way to get fresh produce. There is only so many cans of peaches I can eat. And what are you going to do, it's not stealing, so we take what we need until there is no more. Thankfully I found a medium-sized cooler to keep the frozen stuff as frozen as it could be until I ate it.

I spot some cows who don't seem worse for wear as they are out and grazing with access to shelter for the winters. It is astonishing how resilient animals are and resourceful when need be. There may be some chickens, as I swivel my head like an owl trying to get different vantage points around the property from my perch.

After about a half hour of my owllike behavior and observations, I decide to go take a closer look. Don't want to intrude if someone still lives here or has recently taken ownership, so I drive slowly and honk the horn a couple of times. As I get closer I can see a vehicle parked by the house but no people emerge from the house to check out the noise.

I park my car and take a deep breath. This is exciting and scary and lonely but I overcame so much over the last years I know I can handle this. I exit the car and I hear the crunch of my shoe stepping out into the gravel driveway, but my eyes are feasting on a beautiful simple home and my heart skips a beat. I really hope there is electricity and water 'cause this is my home now. I don't possess any skills to fix any of the electrical or plumbing issues if needed, but I guess I could find a book.

Once I am fully emerged from the car, "Hello, anyone here?" I say in a more confident voice than I actually feel. I almost half expect zombies at this point. I'd die right there from freight or at least pee myself. No response and no zombies, first good sign. I gather up my courage, close and zip my jacket because it's cold out here and it will be cold in there, and make my way into the house.

*Starting Again*

The structure still looks good, and my first priority is to check the lights. My heart skips a beat when the entryway is illuminated with a soft hue of the yellow-brown light from the lightbulb. It is around five p.m. by the time I did the rest of my walk around and ended up at the back porch looking at the beautiful mountain view. I felt grounded and I instantly loved the place. No heebee jeebee vibes and best of all there is a lake in my line of sight, which made my stomach fill up with butterflies. I decided to spend the night.

# Chapter 3

## Everett

I am finishing up mending some of the fence on the left-hand side of the property. It is sunny this afternoon and even though it isn't hot, manual labor in the sun made this man sweat. I tied up my long hair to keep it out of my face with some twine that I found in the trailer of my truck. Not sure if I could get cancer again, but I think a bit of sun exposure is good for my mental health.

I had arrived at this place about six months ago from up island where I grew up. Nothing holding me to my hometown. And growing up only the rich people lived this close to Victoria, so I thought, why not. I stroked my beard as I took a minute's break, not used to the beard so I played with it all the time. Human touch, even if it is my own touch.

Head tilted back to expose as much skin to the sun, I left my mind to wander a bit. This place had felt like home the minute I set foot on the land. I said I would go out and find whatever spoke to me, this place spoke to me. It felt safe and as much like home as a new place could. There were already animals and such, it was a working farm before. The closest neighbor also is a farm, and I fed the animals there as well. In a few days I'll move them over to this farm, I think, make my life easier.

In the mist of my daydreaming, thinking of how to move the cows and the chickens and goats, I heard a car horn, probably some cats in the barn, too, and see how the equipment still works. "Wait, what? Car horn, did I just really hear a car horn?" Saying it out loud brought my mind, thoughts, and focus back to the present, away from the future. It was faint, so faint it could have been in my daydreams. Sounded like it had come, if it was real and not my imagination, from the house next door. I was as close as I could get to it from this side of the fence, so I hopped over and thought I would go look. Somewhere deep down, in the chambers of my heart, I almost hoped it was people. It is beautiful here, but the immense absence of human life makes me claustrophobic.

The healthy grass crunched under each step I took as I closed the gap between where I had been standing to where I had "heard a car horn." There is a little shed blocking my direct view of the house and so I sidestepped to get a better view. That's when I see her, standing on the back porch. Must have been close to five p.m. as the sun is starting to do its dance of what is better known as a sunset, and the brightness dulled just a bit but not enough to cause you blindness if you looked straight into it.

She didn't see me, for a moment or two I am frozen in place, not believing my eyes and then hid behind the shed. Not sure why I did that, I'm not a monster and I have spent most of my life with other humans successfully. But I did and like a twelve-year-old boy I peered around the corner of the shed.

In those two moments I took in a general description of the woman who seemed to be admiring the view of the mountains, so she is distracted enough not to see me. I am essentially staring at her, I could see she is about my age, between forty and forty-five is my guess. Strikingly beautiful long brown hair, loose and hanging down over her shoulders. Average height, but from this distance she could be ten feet tall.

As I stared, really not being able to see the finer details, something felt strange inside me. Like my heart beat twice and then there is a tugging feeling. I didn't want to look like a stalker, and normally I would pop out from behind the shed to introduce myself. But I thought about that scenario again and played it in my head. If I was her I would have a heart attack if out of nowhere a strange man popped out from behind a shed he was clearly watching her from. So I decided to run away, that's right, a grown man tucked down and ran away.

When I made it back out of sight, I decided I would run over tomorrow if she is still there and try not to scare her to death with my presence.

The rest of the day and evening were shot. I couldn't concentrate with the thought of meeting a person in the morning. My knee wouldn't stopping jiggling while I ate, I fidgeted with the pages of my book. "What is wrong with me!" I closed the book and decided to go to bed. No point in pacing nervously, best try to sleep off my nerves.

On my way to bed I passed a mirror in the hallway, hadn't paid much notice to my hair or beard in a while, looked a bit too much like Tom Hanks in *Cast Away* at the present moment. I'd fix it up a bit, I had time. Am I trying to impress the woman? It had been a very long time since I had been with a woman. I am, nor have I ever been married, but I'm not ugly, so before all this went down I had a normal sex life. Hadn't had much time to think about sex, with a person that is. It's been what almost five years. "Shit, five years," I said to Tom staring back at me in the mirror. Maybe I'm not nervous, just hopeful. Maybe.

I trimmed all around. I had come to like my hair and beard, so trimmed the beard but didn't shave it. Not a five-o'clock shadow at all but not more than an inch long. I stood in front of the mirror with the towel around my waist, fresh from the shower as I trimmed my hair. I noticed I am smiling. What a strange thing to do. But there it is, a smile.

    I finished up with my hair and beard, and had planned on putting away the scissors when a thought had occurred to me, and so I followed that thought with my eyes down and took a peak at how long the hair is down there. Again, stupid thought to have but figured while I am cleaning myself up, might as well manscape. The stupidness of it all made me giddy. Off to bed with me, she probably wouldn't be there in the morning.

# Chapter 4

## Charlie

There must have been a rooster in the horde of chickens I saw yesterday evening while standing on that porch, 'cause something is cock-a-doodle-ling, loudly, waking me up. I looked at my watch and read eight a.m. with my hazy eyes. Not bad, remembering that I had gone to bed probably at eight p.m. the night before. That is twelve hours of sleep. And a good sleep at that.

I stretched, and by stretched I mean I cracked my body in various places before swinging my legs off the bed. I had a sleeping bag with me but found a bed that is in pretty decent condition. The combo suited me just fine. There is a fireplace and some nice dry wood inside that kept me and the house warm all night. I sat on the edge of the bed facing a window, letting the sun rays hug my face. My mind thinking of what to do, where to start. I need to take stock of animals, animal food, what tools I have, running water by the barns, there's a man walking across the field, what human food there is and does any of the barns need fixing. "Wait there's a man walking across the field?" Had my mind betrayed me? I bolted into an upright position and am stiff like a board.

I had not felt unsafe when meeting other people on those few occasions, to which I could count on one hand, but this is a bit different and I am not familiar with my surroundings yet. I did a double take to see if he is walking over wielding a knife to kill me, and there is something in his hand. But I couldn't see it. Panic set in, survival mode engaged, and legs finally started moving. What do I have to protect myself? I'm not prepared for this. This just didn't happen anymore. I stumbled around, tripping over my own feet trying to put clothes on and get myself to the kitchen downstairs to find a weapon of my own.

My feet betrayed me in the worst way, and at the worst possible moment, tripping me down the flight of stairs. I landed hard on my side and I screamed involuntarily in pain. I was immobilized, I must have broken a foot and rib, those were to the two areas of greatest pain when I tried to get up.

"Are you all right?" A voice pierced my mind's self-assessment of the damage I just had caused myself. I let out a scream fit for a horror movie, but that is it, I am so scared no words came out. Just a horrific scream and a stare. If he is there to kill me and wear my skin as a swimsuit, I didn't give much reason not to.

"Are you all right? Is anything broken? I'm not here to hurt you, I'm just your neighbor."

He is moving towards me and all I could do is stare. As he got a bit closer I could see that he didn't have a knife in his hand but a flashlight. I relaxed a little, each muscle, one at a time. Relaxed feelings were then quickly replaced with pain feelings, and my face must have contorted with the pain because he ran the last little bit of distance between us and knelt down next to me.

He brought his face in a little closer to mine to start touching areas to see if they hurt. He is beautiful: sharply defined jawline, nose, and cheekbones. Full lips, soft brown thick hair, and a clean contouring beard. The hair had fallen into his face when he bent down and it semi covered his striking jade-green eyes and his doe-like eyelashes.

When his hand touched my hand, a shock of electricity ran up arm and straight into my heart. As if it isn't beating fast enough.

"Can you talk? Are you okay? Can you tell me if you are hurt?"

Pain is quickly replaced with embarrassment that I had fallen down the stairs in the face of what I thought was an attack. I could feel the blood rushing to my cheeks and I mustered a short answer of "I'm okay."

"Are you sure? That sounded like a pretty epic fall." As he said that his nurse-like hands assessing for damage reached my foot, the one that I thought was broken and gave it a little squeeze.

"Ah, oh, well, that hurt a little," I said, and contorted my face again.

"Okay, well, that feels sprained. Can you wiggle your toes?" His eyes looking directly into mine, his hand still on my foot. I am now acutely aware that I am still in my pj's, my hair is a mess I'm sure, I haven't brushed my teeth and this incredibly attractive man is inches from my face and body. He smells clean and fabulous.

"Toes, can you wiggle them?" he repeats himself this time looking more concerned. "Did you hit your head, are you able to focus and tell me your name?"

*Okay, focus up here, Charlie, two questions, you can answer two questions.* "Yes, to wiggling my toes and no to hitting my head. Name is Charlie. Who are you?" Sounding way snippier than I had intended to.

"I'm Everett. I guess you can say I'm your neighbor, live just next door. I was and guess still am a rescue specialist with the Canadian Navy, so not a doctor but have seen it all. If you can wiggle your toes that is good, really is a sprain. Anything else hurt?"

*Stop looking at me with those eyes, I just can bare it anymore*, my mind speaks to him but only I can hear. I wither a bit in my elegant position on the floor. I am just so grateful for underwear, that's all I can think. "Umm. My side, the side I landed on so gracefully is sore."

"Can you take a big breath or does that hurt?"

I take a big breath and no pain, but to the touch it is sensitive. "No, just sore I guess."

"Can I see? And are you okay if I check it out with my hand?"

*You can check out whatever you like, Mr. Everett.* Thankfully that is just in my head to myself. I did manage to shake my head in a yes motion. Jeez, I'm so suave.

Everett moved to get into a better position, he is wearing a plaid buttoned shirt with a vest over it. In his movement his shirt opened up just a little, like a personal peep show, and I saw some very appealing chest hair wave hello. Just enough, and the same color as his hair and beard. If you asked me what name of the color it is, I would have answered *touchable*, but in reality a soft light brown.

I am so focused at looking in and down his shirt, I forgot he is lifting up my shirt to see my ribs, and best of all his hands were all over my skin. I slowly looked down at the touch, it is so warm and welcomed. His fingers were rough but not in a bad way, in an exceptionally good way. It is like having someone run their nails along your back, a little scratchy can go a long way. Little bursts of electricity started to fire in all parts of my body to all the other parts of my body.

He moved in closer, his cheek settled so close to mine. I inhaled a little of his fragrance, trying not to be suspicious but OH MY GOD he smelled nice, like soap and man. I thought I saw him take a sniff of me at the same time I did, but I could be wrong. Why would anyone else be acting like absolute fool other than me? And

*Starting Again*

I really hoped he didn't sniff me as I hadn't showered or cleaned in a few days. Maybe he is sniffing and it isn't good.

"How's that?" he asked me in a very soothing low voice.

"Hmm?" I am brought back to the present and stared at him blankly.

"When I push here what's the pain, between one to ten, ten being horrible?"

"Oh, not bad, probably a five." I smiled back at him, desperate to get up now. I all of a sudden need to get up and distance myself. His presence being so close to me is now intensely overwhelming.

I reached for the railing to help myself get up; he still had a hand on me providing a bit of stability to my side. I stood and straightened myself and my scant amount of clothing. Forgetting I had just fallen down the stairs, I put pressure on my foot to move away from the scene of the crime and Everett. "Oh, that didn't feel good."

Thankfully his hand had never left my body so he caught me as I buckled under the pain. I lifted my foot instinctively.

"You okay, you got it?"

"Eh, ya I think so. Ya, thank you, I'm good."

"You are going to have to stay off your foot for a bit." Everett looked at me but with a blank stare really. I guess he is thinking but as I stood there really wishing he would go away so I could clean up but also stay at the same time and dirty me up, my brain was in no position to make accurate assumptions of what another human was doing.

"You really shouldn't put any weight on it for a bit. Ice and heat. And definitely no stairs. If you want, and this is totally just in a friendly neighbor Canadian Navy way, I could come back and help with food and navigating around. I have to finish fixing the fence but I could come in and check on you at breaks."

"Oh, no, really that is okay. I'll be okay. Really. I just need a shower and some clean clothes and I'll be right as rain."

"Okay, let me see you try to put on an imaginary sock!"

"Copy that, El Capitane." But as Everett already knew, that would be more challenging than I had anticipated, so eventually I caved in and took him up on his offer. I liked the way he smiled when I said that I would probably need his help after all.

"Before I leave let me help you with getting showered and dressed. Bathroom upstairs or this floor?"

"Upstairs." I am not going to argue with this statuesque of man standing in front of me. Now that I am standing I could see he is probably about six feet tall and had a nice slender body. He is tying up his hair to help me and I couldn't help notice how he tied his hair down and not up, no man bun. I liked it either way.

"Okay, ready?"

I stretched out an arm to him and the day began with more human touch than I had had in years. I hope this trend would continue. But for now, like a full gentleman, I am helped into the bathroom and left alone to shower, but he stayed at the door just in case. I put on my own bra and underwear and Everett helped with the shirt and pants. I am helped back downstairs and finally left alone to ruminate on the morning's excitement and plan the next couple of days not being mobile. I decided to journal and read and just be until Everett would come back around lunch. He said my name when he left, my heart liked that.

# Chapter 5

# Together

I'm with the Canadian Navy, look at me, blah blah blah. Everett repeated this in his head in a mocking tone. "Such an idiot," he said outside his head a few times, too. His fence mending is done aggressively with the thoughts of what he said, feeling he looked like a fool. Needless to say, that the fence got repaired very efficiently that morning, much faster than the day before.

*Oh my god, those legs, that body and the hair and the eyes,* was Everett's internal monologue as he fell victim to remembering Charlie, as much as he could remember. She is incredibly beautiful, with long chestnut-brown hair, a bit curly. Deep brown eyes that looked into his soul and they were kind to what they saw. Thin lips, the complete opposite to his and they intrigued him. From what he could tell from the body he could see pre- and post-shower, slender and healthy, and he tried not to stare but had noticed that when he was checking her side that her nipples had become hard and were casting a shape in the material of her shirt.

Everett didn't get a full erection at the thought of her nipples but there were stirrings going on down there. After the shower, in her bra and underwear . . . come on, she was killing him. It took all his strength to be a gentleman. She is very attractive and it is his absolutely pleasure to go back and make lunch to see her again.

Everett worked hard to get as much done by lunch, and sweaty and dirty is the way Charlie was about to experience him. No time for anything else, back to work after lunch so freshening up would have to be closing his jacket.

As he worked, Everett could see Charlie's silhouette in the window. She hadn't really moved from the couch, which is good, means she had listened to him. And as he is making his way over to make food he wondered if she had some or if he is supposed to bring some. She looked up from her book and smiled at him, so too late to turn around now. He would scamper back if needed.

He had thought about coming over all night, hadn't slept all that much but it was all worth it when he first saw her. Yes, it wasn't a good first introduction but it could have been worse. It brought all kinds of feelings, feelings he had not expected. Giddy was one of them, giddy at the prospect of human interaction, physical interaction. Now standing at the door, daydreaming had to be pushed aside, as he knocked on the door.

He opened it, not wanting her to get up to open it and said a quick quiet, "Hello, it's me, Everett, from next door." Seemed to be redundant since there is no one else around for, well probably not until Victoria which is over twenty kilometers away. *Stupid stupid stupid!* Stupidest thing to say, regretting it as soon as it left his mouth.

Charlie didn't make any remarks, thankfully, other than to welcome him in. He took his boots off at the door and followed the voice to where she is sitting.

*Starting Again*

"Hi! How's the foot? And I had a thought on my way here about food, I'm happy to make or bring some, but wasn't sure what the situation was here."

"Oh, I brought a bunch of stuff with me from along the drive. I was lucky enough to find some stores that still have some edible stuff. All of it is in the fridge and freezer. Please help yourself. I'll sit with you, if you don't mind helping me get up and I can get myself to the table."

Mind, oh he didn't mind, any reason to get close and touch Charlie. He did get close and touch Charlie and stole a sniff of her fragrance. Soap and woman, his favorite. "Here, let me, not a problem at all."

"Thanks for making food and fussing over me. Been a while since I was fussed over by another person. It is also nice to speak out loud."

Everett smirked at that; he had had the same thought about just being around people. It is nice to hear that she liked it, that she liked it when he is around, albeit twice in their first day meeting.

They chatted over lunch enjoying the food that Everett prepared, probing for small details about the other and their past. The usual: What kind of cancer did you have? Married? Kids? What brought you to this area? Everett could see Charlie physically get more comfortable with him. She brought her leg up when they were sitting at the table and leaned her chin on her knee, she smiled more and he enjoyed hearing her laugh.

Everett noticed she had a scar in her eyebrow, right side, and her lip curled like Elvis when she is expressing that she didn't like something. He learnt that she had liver cancer, no kids or husband. Looking for somewhere quiet to spend her days and farm. Originally from the US and had only broken one bone. This is amazing to Everett as he had broken several, mostly as a child but a few bones here and there as a full-grown man.

Charlie asked about his career with the Canadian Navy, and listened so intently, Everett thought her eyes were glued to his. Charlie kept asking more and more questions and Everett loved sharing the answers. He had loved being a rescue specialist and captain for the Canadian Navy, maybe he would go back one day. This is just where he needed to be right now. Maybe to heal, but his head isn't in the right space to save others.

Everett went back to the fence for the last couple hours of the day, didn't want to seem over eager. But they did make arrangements for him to come back for dinner. Everett liked the thought of having another meal with Charlie, he liked her and he felt the same feeling coming from her. Even though he is attracted to her physically, it is simply nice to talk to someone.

## Chapter 6

### Together

Everett knocked on the door at five p.m., Charlie thought to herself that he is punctual. The opposite of her. She is not ready yet but would have to make do since he is at the door. She hobbled over to the door and an involuntary smile spread from ear to ear when she saw his handsome face peering in the door window. She opened the door and invited in the stranger she wanted to get to know better.

His hair is down and that just stirred all kinds of desire within her. He wore a hunter-green cotton long-sleeve shirt with a rounded neckline. She saw a peak of his chest hair again, which is fabulous, but the shirt also accented his muscular collarbone and adjacent muscles that attached to it. To Charlie, that is one of the sexiest parts of a man, and in Everett's particular case, his just made it so inviting to touch. She wondered if he had done that on purpose.

His shirt also hinted to strong arms and shoulders and that delicious V shape at his waist. He had on jeans and, most surprising, he is holding some flowers. "Is this a date?" Charlie said out loud to herself to her own surprise. They were beautiful field flowers, few in numbers as it isn't the season, but just enough to melt her heart at the thoughtfulness.

Charlie feels grateful for having put on a dress, even if it is made of sweatshirt material, at least it showed off her freshly shaven legs. She felt underdressed and unprepared compared to Everett. But she guesses she would forge on!

"These are for you! Way better, I think, than a flashlight, but less useful," Everett said, taking off his boots. In her head, Charlie wondered what would be useful to get into Everett's pants but said nothing and smiled.

"I wondered about the flashlight and had forgotten to ask about it this morning and lunchtime." Charlie raised the question as she lowered herself into a chair to watch at the kitchen table.

"Well, the power lines out here I have discovered tend to be very sensitive, and add a little wind and out goes the electricity. Didn't want you to be without any light if that happened in your first couple of days."

Charlie stood up, grunting lightly under her breath, and she rummaged for a vase while Everett talked about the electricity. *He's making electricity in my nether regions that's for sure,* again in her head. Slightly embarrassed for her internal crassness, for how she is sexualizing him. "Stop it!" snuck out as she scolded herself.

"Umm, what? Is there something wrong with the vase?" Everett stopped what he was doing and asked inquisitively.

That last sentence apparently wasn't in her head and embarrassment flushed her cheeks again. "Oh, sorry, no internal monologue. Go on about the electricity, and thank you for the flashlight. That was very thoughtful of you."

"Ya, no worries, happy to be a friendly neighbor. Speaking of which, want me to light a fire?"

"That would be amazing. Thank you," Charlie replied, incredibly grateful for the offer. She could hobble to the fireplace but with a bummed foot it is nice to avoid the hassle. "Spaghetti and plain sauce okay for supper?" Charlie is capable of doing at least that even though the premise of him being there again is to do this for her. Her socked feet would make good sliders and pivoters around the kitchen for at least one meal.

"Sounds perfect. Did you find any of that here?" Everett asked with genuine curiosity.

"Um, no. Stuff I brought with me," Charlie called back to him over her shoulder.

They both set to work on their tasks, leaving a few minutes of silence while Everett started the fire and Charlie searched for pots and started the water. For Charlie, at least, did not find the silence awkward at all. It is nice to know there is someone else in the next room and for now that is all that is needed.

Upon Everett's return to the kitchen, Charlie had set out some candles to go with the flowers. "Is it weird to have candles? I just thought they would go nice with the flowers to fancy up the joint a bit."

"Not weird at all, I like it."

In the dimming light outside and in the candlelight inside, Everett's eyes took on a brooding tone. He had thick eyebrows, not caveman thick, just not pretty-boy manicured. They suited his face and right now they made his eyes look hungry. Charlie isn't sure what to make of all of this. Is she seeing things because she had not seen or been around humans for a while? Or did Everett's look reflect that he is as attracted to her as she is attracted to him.

"Can I ask you something? And please don't let it weird you out, but I'm just not sure anymore about social conduct or behaviors. But is this like sort of a date?" The question stung her mouth as soon as it left her lips. This is a dumb question and since Everett didn't answer immediately she had so much regret. "Never mind, it was a really stupid question, just friendly neighbors sharing a meal."

"Well, I am hoping it is a date, otherwise the flowers are wasted." And with that Everett sent a smile her way, full teeth, and what beautiful teeth he had. And a little wink.

*Oh I'm in trouble,* Charlie thought to herself. "Okay, well good then. I didn't put a dress on or shave my legs for nothing. Not really shaved my legs as much as ran a dry razor up and down a couple of times." Charlie ended that with a nervous laugh.

"Listen, I don't know about how all this works now either. But we can make this our own, either way. Let's just keep an open dialogue and see where that takes us. And if it makes you feel any better, I trimmed my beard for you, so we are even on the hair maintenance."

They both gave out a little giggle and that seemed to cut the tension as they both visibly relaxed. Shoulders came down, facial muscles relaxed. It is good. It is great, actually.

"Oh, and I found some wine. I don't drink but can I offer you some?" Charlie offered.

"As long as it doesn't bother you, sure I'll have just a glass."

"Great let me get you one!"

Over the next couple of hours they dined and chatted and laughed. Enjoyed each other's company. Stealing little glances here, a brush of hand as they walked past each other. It is obvious that they both liked each other and that they both really wanted to have sex with each other. *Very obvious.* They were like magnets, slowly drawing closer to each other. At first they sat in the living room opposite to each other and each time someone got up for a real or made-up reason, they chose a closer spot.

Everett ran out quickly, interrupting their flow a bit but the animals needed feeding and their customary turn-down service.

By around ten p.m., it is dark as black outside, the candles had been moved into the living room to cast a romantic spell on all that lay within a few feet of them. There is an intense electricity between them, neither are even paying attention to what the other is saying. Words left their mouths, but recognition of the human language is not registering.

Everett could no longer hold back his desire or at least ignore it and blurted out, "I really want to kiss you!"

Charlie is a little taken aback but as she is being honest with herself she had wanted to ask or jump right in for the last couple of hours. "I don't know how this goes. Well . . . you know . . . I know how sex goes, I'm not a virgin, but this, this interaction. I only met you today and I don't want to come off as easy but I really do want to kiss you, too. So I'm glad you said something, thank you for that. But, ummm, can we take it slow like kiss and see how it goes?"

Everett isn't turned off by Charlie's ramblings about taking it slow. He knew deep down that he wasn't really expecting sex tonight. Kissing and making out sounded like the best place to start and see how everyone feels. "I'm good with taking it slow, since I don't know how this all plays out either. But I do know that I want to figure it out with you. I like you, Charlie. I've had the best time just getting to know you over the last twelve hours. And I really hope we can keep doing that again tomorrow."

Charlie liked what she heard, really liked what she is seeing and really wanted to taste his mouth more than anything in the world. It felt right and she is positive it would feel good.

It is as if he read her consent and permission on her face. Everett stepped towards her but only about seventy-five percent of the way, leaving the remaining twenty-five percent for Charlie to close the gap and to say a definite "yes." And she did without hesitation. This little dance they did fueled their mutual attraction to each other, when they had closed the gap completely Everett reached with his hand and gently grabbed Charlie's head from the back, cupping it more than grabbing, pulling her face to his.

Their lips connected, hands found something to touch or to hold onto or to pull closer. At first their lips were gentle, gentle explorers, and just lips. Charlie wanted more. She parted her lips to show Everett she is wanting more. More of him. Everett picked up what Charlie is laying down and, in sync, parted his lips and greeted her tongue with his.

There is passion and a little of desperation, mixed with a whole lot of loneliness behind the gentle exchange of touches. Whatever feelings had been held hostage inside their singular existence up until this morning, they were crying with relief with the heat of their hands on skin, with the pleasure that radiated throughout their whole bodies.

Charlie sucked in Everett's lip and nibbled it a bit before letting it go. That was the first time in the last three minutes that their lips parted. Their hands were still holding each other's bodies close. Everett is filled with mixed feelings. Mindful that he is starting to get an erection and didn't want to scare Charlie but he is reveling in her closeness. He rubbed his nose gently along hers, her skin soft and warm. Charlie made it evident she enjoyed kissing Everett and him rubbing his nose along hers.

Everett brushed Charlie's loose, long, and luscious hair from her face to behind her ear. He loved the silkiness of her hair. The color a deep, rich chestnut brown. The tones of her features remind Everett of the forest. Her brown hair and eyes with that olive skin tone.

"I suppose I should leave. I want to respect your wishes and need to get up early to feed the animals."

"My ankle is all better and I need to learn to feed my animals. Can I help you tomorrow so I can learn?"

"Sure, ya, great. I'd love to do that. I usually get up around six a.m. It is not glorious at that hour but by the time I get to everyone it is late in the morning if I don't start early."

Charlie gave Everett her best cute smile and twisted from side to side in place. "Well, I think it would be easier if we woke up together, if you wanted to sleep here. No sex, but I haven't snuggled in a long time. Sure would be nice to fall asleep in your arms."

These are extraordinarily strong feels Charlie is expressing, hoping that Everett felt the same. Sex is sex, but cuddling is intimate.

"Sure, that would be nice. I'll just run back to grab my toothbrush and something more comfortable to sleep in."

Charlie is delighted, a little girl inside her is doing a happy dance. There is just something about Everett that made her feel, well, the best word she could think is whole. It surprised her a little but with the last number of years that humanity had, you don't fool around. You know or you don't know.

# Chapter 7

## Together

While these feelings emerged, and Charlie was trying to decide what to do with them all, she brushed her teeth to free the bathroom for Everett when he came back. It was dark outside so she really couldn't see him, but she saw the light of his flashlight move like a firefly back to his place. A few heartbeats passed and he returned back to her place.

Charlie changed into her sleep attire, which is a loose-fitting T-shirt and booty shorts. She didn't have much in general for clothes and even less choice for sleepwear. Plus, she got hot at night, so nightgowns were not her thing.

Everett returned upstairs in a flash, brushing his teeth in his sleep ensemble, briefs and nothing else. Quite the vision to admire from where Charlie is seated on the bed adjacent to the ensuite bathroom. He is tall, lean, muscular, and sweet. His face, handsome, of course that she already knew, and his hair. Charlie's fingers could get lost in that hair for hours.

Everett finished in the bathroom and turned to leave, facing Charlie now. Charlie, sitting on the edge of the bed, didn't even try to hide that she was admiring his physique just nanoseconds earlier. Everett liked the way Charlie looked at him and took the opportunity to admire her back. She is lean and strong, he liked that healthy body type. He is not sure how he would make the whole night next to her without getting aroused, but he is excited to hold someone, be close to someone without sex. It is intimate and he needed that.

After they had gotten into bed, they felt a bit awkward. It had been a long day so sleep came quickly, especially once they both settled down into a cozy head on chest position. Strange to be cuddling someone you just met and didn't have sex with. Usually the cuddling came after sex with someone you had some sort of connection or deeper feeling for.

They had not known each other long but there is something magnetic to their presence together. Charlie is not scared or worried that Everett would hurt her; Everett is not worried Charlie is a psycho who would murder him in his sleep. So, all in all, they felt good about the situation they were in.

Around four a.m. Everett did wake up from a dead sleep, something pleasant and warm and sensual is massaging his lips. There is a weight on his body, something more than the blanket's weight. The weight is pressed hard on his erection and moving slowly up and down. Feather-like tickles along his face moved up and down in the same rhythm of the weight against his body.

Somewhere between dreamland and awake-land Everett started to move his body to the same rhythm and his hands started to wake up, feeling and searching the weight on top of him. Is he dreaming? He could feel warmth and heat, inside and outside his body. He realized he isn't sleeping and the weight is Charlie on him, grinding her body against his. She is panting oh so lightly, and her rhythm picked up once she sensed Everett is awake and a willing participant.

Everett's erection had awoken her from a pretty solid sleep. Both were probably sleeping well but also aware of each other's presences and their own behaviors. Charlie was semi-conscious and determined not to fart in her sleep. Not on the first sleepover, at least. When Charlie had snuggled in a bit closer to Everett in her sleep, she was the little spoon so had pushed her bum right up against Everett.

Now, not having sex in a while and finding Everett very, very attractive, she became instantly aware of what was going on and decided fairly quickly to seize the opportunity. Early morning shenanigans are for the living and live she shall.

So with carpe diem in her blood pumping throughout her body, she seized the moment. At first she turned over and started softly kissing Everett, they were face-to-face now. It took a few seconds, but it seemed as though he is responding to her advancements. Picking up what she is putting down as the kids say. She nudged him to roll over and mounted this stud. His body felt so good against hers. Her nipples harden in response to the chemical reaction going on in her body and she became wet.

When Everett started moving his hands and pressing his hips against hers to gain more friction in the good area, that flicked Charlie's on button and there is no going back. Charlie sat up, sad to leave Everett's lips and tongue, but she needed desperately to release the hounds so that Everett could have access to her demanding breasts and nipples. Charlie, very happy that Everett sat up to accommodate her needs; his mouth instantly finding her nipples, his hands gently massaging the bounty of her breasts at the same time.

Charlie tipped her head back and let out a whispered moan. Everett moaned as an automatic reply. His erection had gone from morning wood to porn star in that very moment. He is so hard that it felt the like the skin would not hold in the meat together any longer in his shaft. They both still had bottoms of sorts on, and Everett set out to rectify this roadblock, flipping Charlie onto her back and mounted her in one swift movement.

Everett brought his face down slowly and close to Charlie's. "Hi," he whispered with a smile. "Hi," Charlie whispered back with the same sensual smile. It is only a second, but they looked at each other and felt connected and having sex felt like the wrong term for what is about to happen. Making love seemed more appropriate. Satisfied with having made a visual consent, Everett began his journey to Charlie's pleasure center better known as a clit, by kissing his way down her nose, her chin, her neck. Stopping to bite gently and suck her skin. Running his tongue down her neck, along her collarbone. Tasting her skin, her flesh, as he went.

He repositioned his hands along her arms to her hands where he intertwined his fingers with hers, to hold her hands down above her head for as long as he could reach as he stretched his body down hers. Charlie wiggled in pleasure, making sure that Everett knew what he is doing made her feel good and excited.

When he could no longer reach her hands, he let them go and let them meander down to her breasts. Engaging in a sequence of light squeezing, massaging, and pinching her nipples, which were hard and very responsive. Charlie moaned and rocked her hips up and down, back and forth, against Everett's body. Almost like she is trying to shimmy his head down to her blood-filled clit. He is torturing her with his calm journey down her body.

She is desperate to have him fill her, to rock himself inside her back and forth, to enter her with his full, hard erection. She could barely stand the teasing, delicious as it is to have him bring out pleasure through her breasts and his electric kissing. Charlie wanted to have penetration and wanted that from Everett the most.

In her thirty-ish years of being sexually active, she never really felt this safe, this turned on, this ready to have a penis slide into her wet vestibule. She felt passion, and sexy, and connected all at once. She didn't care that she had morning breath or that Everett did, too. She didn't care that she probably had a bit of a pungent smell from marinating all night. She wanted Everett more than anything in the world.

Everett understood what Charlie is asking for, panting for, and went straight in, placing his tongue on her clit and started making circles around it to help the fleshy knob finds its way into his mouth. Charlie spasmed in pleasure, pushing her body upwards into Everett. Everett began to suck and flick the nerve endings with his tongue. He found a pace that Charlie seemed to be most into and kept with it. His hands found their way down, his index finger and middle finger of his right hand, found their way to Charlie's opening, and massaged the edge just a little to bring out some of her wetness. Slipping his fingers all the way in, deep. Keeping them deep to add pressure the entire time he is giving her oral pleasure.

Charlie could barely stop herself from orgasming, every nerve and pleasure sensory is heightened to almost the maximum she could take without orgasming. It has been a while and Everett pushed every right button. Charlie sat up slightly and pushed Everett off her playfully. Everett looking up with a question mark on his face. He asked her, "Do you want to stop?"

"No, I want you in me so badly, now, Everett, now, please."

Everett isn't going to ask twice, the woman said now and please. So now and please is what he is going to give her. His briefs somehow burst off his body, no fuss or muss, freeing him. Both were now completely naked, panting and ready.

Everett handled the shaft of his erection to circle Charlie's opening like his fingers had done to wet the tip of his circumcised head. "Everett," moaned Charlie, and with that Everett entered slowly and carefully at first. Charlie's body welcomed him in by lifting her legs ups, repositioned her hips upwards as well and spread her legs. Widening the welcoming committee.

Everett lowered his body, leaned on his elbows so he could taste her mouth while he slid in and out. Charlie's wetness excited Everett. There is electricity running through his body and with each in, he could feel himself getting closer and closer.

Charlie moved one of her hands down to continue stimulating her clit and the other to squeeze her nipple. Everett moved onto his hands to allow her access and in the early morning pale light he could still see enough. He enjoyed seeing her pleasure herself, and enjoyed feeling her hand pleasure herself some more.

"Everett, I'm close, I'm going to come. Don't stop, faster!"

Everett closed his eyes to focus solely on how she felt around him, she tightened. "I'm going to come, too, you feel so good."

"You feel so good, don't stop, please." It is Charlie's *please* that sent him down the final leg of the race. His thrusts became deeper and faster.

"Yes, like that, yes, yes, yes!" Charlie's head went back and she squeezed a handful of sheets. Her whole body went stiff with an explosion of ecstasy that imploded from the middle of her body outwards to her hands and feet. At the same time, Everett took his final push and groaned, experiencing the same release of ecstasy.

# Chapter 8

## Together

They both lay there, content. The morning sun visible now, spilling a beautiful soft bright pink across the sky like a glass of spilt milk along a countertop. The morning light continued to spill into the bedroom window and over their naked bodies, their breathing returning to normal while Everett still lay on top of Charlie.

As the moment of passion started to fade and reality started making its way in, this left a bit of space for both of them to now realize that they just had sex and they were still naked, and no one had brushed their teeth. All this before coffee. It is a bit to take in.

"That was, umm, unexpected. Wonderful and unexpected." Everett spoke the words but his mind is processing that they had not used any protection. And despite the fact that it is significantly more difficult to make a baby, diseases were still a real thing.

Charlie, coming to the same path in her thoughts said, "It was wonderful, but I guess we should have talked about any issues or

STDs," pointing down with her eyes as she said this. "I'm clean, haven't had sex since I was diagnosed and was screened at that time since being an alcoholic comes with poor decision-making. Anything you need to share?"

Everett laughed, out loud, with a hardy ha ha that came from deep inside. Charlie, slightly confused and scared all at the same time, tilted her head to the side and gave him a suspicious look.

"You have done that a couple of times already; it is like you can read my thoughts. I had the same thought," he said in a reassuring tone, "and I'm clean, too. Same situation, only freaked out with the diagnosis and had a sketchy one-night stand. So I got a clean bill of health after that."

Relief flooded Charlie and she could tell the same happened for Everett. They both were now smiling at each other and the conversation started to flow easily. "That was pretty amazing. I'm not sure what took me over. Glad you hopped on board with the idea," Charlie remarked as she gave a sly chuckle.

Everett moved his body just slightly off Charlie, to the side of her to maintain contact but as not to crush her any longer with his weight. "I found it very hot. I like a woman to take charge every once in a while." And with that he leaned in for kiss, this one not full of sexual passion, but more heart-filled affection. Their lips were still moist from passionate kissing a mere few minutes ago, but this time was softer.

They lay there together for about half an hour, covers pulled up to warm the nakedness of their bodies. Legs and feet twisted like pretzels, Charlie's head on Everett's chest. She listened to his heartbeat. Nice and strong and regular. Everett held Charlie as she lay on him, feeling her soft skin. They did not sleep but merely silently enjoy the closeness, and the extra heat they were cooking up between them.

Charlie is the first to speak. "What did you mean when you said that I spoke what you were thinking, before about, you know, the awkward 'Do you have any sexually transmitted diseases' question?"

"Well, before when you asked if our dinner together was a date. I was wondering that, too."

"Oh, funny. I guess we are on the same wavelengths. Or like my mom used to say *great minds think alike!*"

"Ha, my mom to used to say that, too. Guess it is a mom thing."

Charlie looked up at Everett, he had become more handsome if possible since yesterday. Although, she could smell herself in his beard, so decided that it is time to get up and start the day. "Shall we get up and start the day?"

"Sure. I'll just jump in the shower and get cleaned up. Any chance you want to join me?"

Charlie, intrigued by the question and not that it is an out-there question, just expected it. It made her feel incredibly happy for some reason. Wanted in a lot of ways. "Hmmm, that is an interesting proposal mister . . . mister . . . well, I don't know your last name, Mr. Everett. We have seen each other's naughty parts but I don't know your last name. What is it?"

"Well, Ms. Charlie, my last name is Peterson, and you?"

"Peterson, I like that, Everett Peterson. My last name is Wolfe, Charlie Wolfe."

## Chapter 9

## Together

Charlie usually would be uncomfortable naked around a man she is attracted to, but Everett made her feel desired and perfect just the way she is. On their short journey from the bed to the six feet to the bathroom to take this cleansing shower, Everett had climbed out of bed first, extended his hand out to assist Charlie out of bed, twirled her into his arms with her back to his chest, and he walked them both to the bathroom from behind her. The old hardwood floors creaked with each of their steps.

Everett had made a few noises of admiration when Charlie had been standing in full view. Instead of shying away, Charlie leaned in to the compliments and accepted them just for what they were. That is a first for Charlie and she liked it.

In the shower with the warm water cascading down from head to feet, pooling where their bodies connected, they embraced in each other's arms, now facing each other. The kissing and touching is becoming much more sensual. Slow, tender, and vulnerable.

Everett broke the embrace to wrap his arms around Charlie's shoulders and pull her in closer and tighter. Leaning his head on top of hers, Charlie is in the position to wrap her arms around him as well, tucking her head under his chin for easier access for his kisses on her head.

Charlie looked up and Everett kissed her forehead, water moving likes rivers around his lips and down her face. He moved lovingly down to her nose, moving horizontally to each of her eyes. There is something so caring in his kisses, Charlie couldn't explain how, she just somehow knew that this is good and real. But nothing is guaranteed, and Charlie knew that to be truer than her feelings.

But for right now, she is just going to simply enjoy the moment, the closeness. Lost in her thoughts, she is brought back to reality by Everett kissing her cheeks and now pouncing on her lips with his. Still very tender, but with a hint of spice. The spice turned into fire in thirty seconds flat, but always tender. This isn't as desperate and as needy as in bed. This is passion, compassion, caring, and loving.

Everett ran his hand down to Charlie's leg and lifted it by the knee, making room for him to step in just a bit closer between her legs. His erection is back and he pressed it into her tummy. Standing face-to-face like this, there is a bit of a height difference which had gone unnoticed in bed while lying down. Now in the shower, this could present a bit of a challenge to find the right position for entry.

Everett guided Charlie gently backwards until her back was up against the shower wall. Everett cupped Charlie's breasts, one in each hand. A handful, perfectly perfect because anything more would be a waste. Everett knelt down onto one knee, and his hands slid down, one to brace her hip and the other to spread her

## *Starting Again*

lips to expose her sweet nib of nerves. Groaning with pleasure at the sight in front of him, Everett dove in hungry to pleasure and satisfy Charlie.

Everett ran his tongue along all of her vagina parts, lips inside and out, top to bottom, bottom to top and finally landing on her clit. Remembering the pace and sequence of sucking and flicking that seem to please Charlie the most, Everett mimicked those again for round two.

Charlie took a breath in when Everett started to work on her clit, her hand automatically went to grab a handful of his hair and she squeezed just a little. Everett enjoyed the noise and the action, which made him harder and work harder with his mouth.

In a steady but swift motion, Everett slipped his arms behind Charlie's legs starting from the inner thigh and began to stand up, forcing Charlie to get into the sitting position with her legs slung over Everett's shoulder. As Everett slowly started to stand, Charlie's back slid smoothly along the shower wall. Everything is wet and slippery so it is a fairly comfortable action.

Everett didn't break a beat while pleasuring Charlie orally as he stood up. Bracing himself not to slip by placing a foot on the edge of the tub and holding Charlie by her firm ass, Charlie moaned and groaned deep in her throat, pulling more hair as she steadied herself by holding Everett's head. Initially when Everett started to stand she was a bit scared, but everything he is doing with his mouth is a wonderful distraction from any fear she might have started to feel. He is so good with his tongue and when he picked her up like it is nothing, that made her desires flame.

"Everett, I want you, I want you inside me." Charlie ached for Everett to put his dick inside her. She had never felt so sexual before, she liked how Everett made her feel, how he brought out sides of her that had been hidden for so long.

Everett, aiming to please, slowly putting Charlie down on her own feet. Everett spun Charlie by the shoulders so her back is now facing him. "What do you want me to do to you?" Everett grabbed Charlie's beautiful long hair and tugged it back with a sturdy hand, but not painfully.

Charlie placed her hands on the wall in front of her, as if being frisked by the police, where moments earlier Everett had seated her against with his body. This is vastly different from their early morning escapades, turning a bit primal. She is very turned on; she could feel Everett's hunger for her and his hunger to please her.

She instinctively spread her legs and placed one up on the edge of the tub to allow better access from behind. Everett took her actions as an answer to his question and with his free hand grabbed his hard erection and swirled it in circles at Charlie's opening, just tip-deep to tease her and to bring out her natural lubricant. Charlie arched back in greedy anticipation of the first thrust.

Everett using his hand to guide in his throbbing erection into Charlie, going slowly for about half the way in and a powerful push for the remaining distance. Their bodies connected like a wave crashing against a rock. Charlie threw her head back and let out a gasp of satisfaction.

Everett released Charlie's hair and gripped her hips with his hands but not before he ran his hands down her wet hair clinging to her back and enjoying her warm skin of her lower back. Everett leaned his body against Charlie's to get closer to her ear and he whispered, "You feel so good around me," and he started to slide in and out of Charlie in a slow pace and gradually picking up the speed to match his growing orgasm.

Charlie matched his rhythm and did her own pumping of her hips to get Everett deeper. Charlie left one hand against the wall to keep her balance, but with her now free hand brought it down to her clit to stimulate that part while Everett focused on her g-spot. She uses her index and middle finger to rub that pleasure center, tightening her muscles on the inside of her honeypot when Everett is inside, and relaxing them when he pulls back. Heightening the electricity running through her blood, she could feel her climax growing stronger.

Everett could feel her tightening, and after watching her hand move downwards to rub herself, that threw him into the homestretch. He pumped faster and a bit harder. "Charlie, you are so sexy, I'm close, I'm going to come."

"Come for me, I'm going to come, too. Don't stop, oh fuck!"

Her words finished Everett off, an explosion of energy overtook his body, waves of intense currents radiated throughout his body. Everett felt Charlie go rigid and stop breathing for a second, then takes in a deep breath. Both their bodies went into a Jell-O-like states while they enjoyed the afterglow from "the" release.

The shower water is going cold, which brought them back to earth and interrupted their delighted state. They made a quick exit, fumbling for towels to warm up their cooled skin. Charlie let off a little shiver, which Everett noticed. He pulled her to him to have skin-on-skin contact and wrapped a towel around them both.

"Hi," Everett said while looking deep into Charlie's eyes.

"Hi," Charlie said in response.

"I don't think I'm any cleaner than before the shower." They burst into laughter and hugged each other tight.

"Me either," Charlie snorted. It is Charlie this time to move Everett's hair from his face. He is so handsome, butterflies filled her stomach.

"Shall we get dressed?" Everett said as he released Charlie from his embrace, reaching for his briefs and remaining items of clothing. Charlie nodded in agreement and left him in the bathroom to seek out today's outfit. She decided on jeans and a sweater she found, left from the previous owner. Charlie realized that she hasn't really taken any time to look around and explore the house. She would need to bring the rest of her stuff from the car, too.

"Maybe when we are done with the animals, we can walk around and explore the house and stuff. If you want. Or maybe you could show me your place. I'm happy to do whatever," she spoke with a shy tone, acutely aware that even though she has shared two amazing sexual moments with Everett, they still only met yesterday.

# Chapter 10

## Together

After breakfast they set out to work, cleaning stalls, feeding, milking. Before Charlie started to work, when they had stepped out of the house and onto the back porch, she is struck with the most breathtaking vision. A beautiful mountain range, peaks still covered in snow, bright nourishing sun in shades of a nectarine enveloping the valley from the edge where the earth meets the sky. Closer would be evergreens tall and sturdy as far as the eye could see into a distant forest. The green is the darkest shade found on the hard shell of a watermelon. The sky is clear and if you looked straight up you could see faint stars fading into the baby-blue background.

This is no different than yesterday morning, but Charlie didn't really get to enjoy it on account of falling down the stairs. She thought to herself that tomorrow if it isn't raining she would have her morning coffee on the porch. Charlie hoped Everett would join her.

"Pretty spectacular, isn't it?" Everett had stopped a little distant off the porch when he noticed the absence of Charlie's footsteps.

"I have no words. It is always this nice, the weather, I mean?"

"Well, I've been here six months and it rained almost nonstop up until about April. Seems to be tapering off. The beautiful scenery that is all over Vancouver Island: rainforests, the ocean, the Rockies, and the wildlife, will be interesting to see how this all changes with fewer humans running amok."

"Truly breathtaking. I was just thinking I'd like to have coffee on the porch tomorrow morning, want to join me?" After the question left Charlie's lips she instantly regretted it. It, the question, almost sounded presumptuous that Everett would be around again tonight. Charlie's expression on her face is an outward wince and an inward cringe.

"Sure, love to." And with that Everett went on his way like the question was normal and maybe he wanted to hang out with her again today and tonight, too. Charlie's heart blushed and she stood on the porch and watched Everett walk away. His lean, sexy body striding towards his barn, Charlie couldn't stop herself from thinking about how those strong arms had lifted her whole body in the shower or how she had wrapped her legs around those legs in bed.

She very much liked looking and touching Everett, but she felt a slightly deeper connection to him. She admired what he did before, she felt safe with his background and training, and she realized that they didn't need to fill each moment with talking. And when they did talk, she was genuinely interested in what he had to say. That felt mutual, he seemed genuinely interested when she talked as well.

"Hey, you coming? Is your foot doing okay?" Everett's voice pulled her out of her daydream, greeted by a pleasant smile on his face.

"Oh, ya, sorry. Just lost in watching your butt." With a smirk and a wink, Charlie descended the three stairs off the porch and did a little trot until she reached Everett. Instead of stopping when she reached him, she slapped his butt and tried to sprint away, laughing and giggling.

They played like this all day, taking any opportunity between tasks to touch each other, to look at each other. As they worked they shared more about themselves, childhoods, families, and who had more broken bones up to the current date. Everett won with a broken thumb from skateboarding, wrist from surfing, and rib while working for the navy. Charlie had only broken a toe playing soccer as a kid. But she won in the *who had more scars* game.

Around lunchtime the chores were all done, on both sides. Everett had shared what he had learned about this routine, and having lived in farm country, Charlie already knew a thing or two, which she shared with Everett. It is easy to talk to Everett, the conversation just flowed, and it seemed the same for Everett and he actively participated in sharing and describing his life before the shit hit the fan.

Charlie also realized as they were talking, because the subject is getting closer and closer to both of them having had cancer and what story each had, that she had not once thought about drinking. Or felt any emotions about it at all since meeting Everett. That is nice. It is exhausting to be constantly reminded of the urge to drink, so it is a nice mental break.

Since it has only been about a year, a little less, since really all food production stopped, fresh fruits and veggies were not readily found. That year, the focus really was dealing with the dead. Most of the meals were canned or something frozen. Flours and such survived and so did non-dairy products. This morning Charlie made pancakes using eggs from Everett's chickens. Lunch will be canned soup and crackers, and dinner would probably pasta be again. They would have to go out and see if they could do a food run in town or in Victoria.

Everett rubbed Charlie's feet with his own as they sat and ate their lunch. The socks rubbing together physically charged them and when Charlie reached over to touch his arm she gave Everett a surprisingly good shock. They both laughed over the hilarity of Everett jumping almost out of his chair. "It is nice to laugh with another human being. Been awhile since I heard another person's laugh. It's usually just mine I hear," Everett said, then the laughing had subsided.

Everett loved Charlie's laugh, it is not fake and it seems to come from the belly. It is contagious and beautiful. Charlie is beautiful. Everett studied her face and how she moved. Charlie is very expressive when talking especially about something she is passionate about. She had laugh lines around her mouth and eyes, they were simply perfect.

Everett waited until Charlie had finished her storytelling of when she was a little girl and her dad had taken her hunting with him. Everett is listening but only partially because now he had a question he wanted to ask and it seemed to be consuming his attention at the moment. When Charlie had finished, Everett gave a three-second pause to make sure he isn't interrupting, and when it felt safe, "Hey. So, random question for you. I'm forty-one, how old are you? I am just admiring how beautiful you are and the question started burning a hole in my brain."

"I am wondering the same but didn't want to be rude and ask." Charlie is fully joking and gave a smile quickly after so that Everett would know as much. "Just kidding, I am thinking about it, but I don't think it is a rude question at all. I'm forty-three years young and not ashamed of my age!"

"Oh, I'm sleeping with an older woman, my favorite porn search!" Everett also joked and thought it appropriate to get a little humor revenge. And also quickly smiled to make sure Charlie knew that he is just kidding. "Also just kidding. When is your birthday?"

"It was a couple of days ago, May 2. And you?"

"Well, first, happy belated birthday, we will have to celebrate. And second my birthday is August 18. What date did you go into full remission, what's your *I survived cancer* date?" Everett's smile as he talked melted Charlie's heart.

"Believe it or not mine is my birth date. I celebrated my forty-first birthday cancer-free. It is such a mind fuck that only cancer victims survived the world's twenty-fourth major pandemic only to watch everyone else that they love and know die. How about you, what is your cancer-free date?" Charlie replied.

"April 27, and I don't know about you but watching everyone I love die with not a hope in hell to be saved because the vaccine was rushed and not effective, has left me with a good-sized amount of survivor's guilt. I am torn every day between being grateful and feeling guilty. That I better do something amazing with the gift of life that I was given and then feel like that I shouldn't enjoy life because my family and friends cannot. That's why I came here, I needed to get away from all the reminders of all that I have lost, in hopes to rebuild the life I dreamt of while dying."

Everett seemed a bit lost in his thoughts, and he clearly looked emotional to Charlie. While he was talking she had moved to him to help comfort him with her closeness. "I feel that way, too. I would find it hard to believe if any of us survivors didn't feel that way. We all have the same story to a certain extent and human nature would dictate that most, if not all, would feel guilty for being the ones to live. Taking the population from eight billion to eighteen million will leave a scar on us all."

Everett hadn't noticed that Charlie had moved, but when she spoke to him he is brought back to the present from the past and, without thinking, put his arm around her waist and squeezed her close. Everett has spent a life witnessing death and tragedies and humans at their worst, but as senseless as that was, the senselessness had never affected the ones he held dear.

Charlie is not weirded out by Everett's need of her, of bringing her closer. It in fact just reinforced all the feelings she had had before. It just seemed to feel right, Everett felt right, and them together felt right. In turn, Charlie wrapped her arms around his neck and held him until his grip started to loosen.

"Sorry. Didn't mean to take our chat into a dark dungeon. The dark dungeon of my thoughts and feelings. I felt only sadness before, but now that I have met you, I am grateful you survived and found your way here. And that I survived and was here to be found," Everett spoke into her arm.

# Chapter 11

## Together

The unloading of a tiny bit of what Everett was holding deep down in the deepest spaces of his psyche, made him feel freed. He isn't skipping around saying how light on his feet he felt, but it is more like just being aware of the absence of those feelings of depression. Every day may not feel like this, but Everett decided to just enjoy this moment right now.

After lunch they walked around, inspecting the barns and sheds on Charlie's property. She had cats that had survived on mice, goats that survived eating all vegetation in the fenced-in area, chickens who probably survived on feed and grains they found as they wandered around the barns. No animals were trapped inside the barns, which was good as they could seek food and water wherever available on the property. The property itself is fenced in but that stretched out on many acres. Plus, the barns were in excellent condition, so they had shelter in the colder days.

It is amazing to see how nature had continued on, wouldn't say survived necessarily, but it didn't perish. Maybe with less people it will return to a more balanced state.

Everett helped Charlie bring her belongings from her car into the house. They explored each room, taking things that she wanted to keep or move to another room. Removing personal items that made it creepy to be in this home, like the family's photos and cards. It would take a few weeks, but all clothing would be sorted to keep or get rid of. They would go through the pantries and throw away anything that is not edible. Replace them with her things, her identity.

Charlie had noted mentally during their walk that the style of the home suited her, or at least didn't violently repulse her, so nothing had to be done right away. No out-of-date colors like olive green or caramel, very neutral and easy on the senses. Nothing lavish or gaudy, it is sensible and everything had a purpose.

They joked around with each other, even held hands here and there. It felt like they were settling nicely into a relationship but didn't know each other at all, or very little. They took as many opportunities as they could to steal glances, to sneak a soft touch. Charlie let her hair fall in her face throughout the entire day in hopes that Everett would brush it back behind her ear with care, leaving her face wide open for a kiss. And Everett enjoyed obliging her silent requests once he caught on to what she was doing.

The more they explored the house, the more Charlie was making a connection with it. The previous owners seemed to align with Charlie's sense and style; everything served a purpose and she could feel it was loved. She could feel love and she could feel how cherished the memories made here were.

"It's strange but I feel a connection to the house. Isn't that strange to feel connected to an inanimate object? But, I do." Charlie had found herself sharing with Everett at the end of their day, standing in the kitchen together having some tea before making dinner.

"Ya, a bit strange but I understand completely. I felt like that about the area while I was searching for a new place to call home. Sometimes the universe just leads you to where you didn't know you needed to be."

"Well, I'm glad we are strange together, in one way or another. Pretty boring to be the only weirdo around! Hey, I'm going to take a shower before dinner, want to join me again? If you don't want to or want to do your own thing I would understand, we have only met like a day ago." Charlie hoped with her entire body that Everett didn't want to be on his own or go back to his place. Charlie hadn't realized her whole body had tensed up with the question until Everett said he'd love to continue hanging out with her. Her whole body dropped back down to the earth about an inch after he said that.

"But if you don't mind, I'll let you shower and I'll go back to my place and do that same, grab some clothes and some food, come back here. Maybe tomorrow we can stay at my place."

Charlie is overjoyed with the future invitation, and tickled pink that Everett seemed as into her as she is into him. "That would be nice, I would love to see your place." And with that, Charlie said nothing else. She did want to say that she would bring some stuff to sleepover in, but felt that would be too presumptuous. She would just see how everything unfolded tomorrow.

"All right, then, you go up and shower and I'll be back in twenty minutes or so. Deal?"

"Deal!"

They parted ways, a smile plastered on their faces left for only new lovers in the throes of an exciting new love. They both raced to do the things they needed to do to get back to each other's company.

# Chapter 12

## Everett

I have no idea what has come over me, but I find myself racing to shower and grab my stuff to get back to Charlie. The last two days have been exciting and comforting and a semblance of pre-pandemic. It felt good and I am enjoying it.

Charlie is amazing, easy to talk to, and I enjoy when she shares little bits of her life with me. I love that she feels comfortable around me and I love that neither of us seem to be acting for the other. What point would acting get us, we are probably the only two people in five hundred kilometer radius and that is only because we are close to a big city. This second chance at life has really changed the remaining humans in a major way.

For now it seems that no major decisions are being made about jobs and work and what to do with all the empty businesses or how people are taking what they need. Everyone seems to be accepting of each other and their differences. Not being attached to our phones or the internet has helped my anxiety tremendously and I'm sure I'm not alone. We, as a whole, just seem more relaxed. I am purely basing that on my experience and what I hear from some friends and distant relatives.

I want to be with Charlie and share this new moment in history with her. I want to make history with her. And it is not purely based on the spectacular sex, which I also hope with all my heart continues, it feels like this goes deeper. Out of a sparse eighteen million, I feel grateful for the first time in years that she ended up here.

These are deep thoughts to be having while showering, but I want to be clean for the lady in the house next door. Eat and be merry and forget for a few minutes longer all that we have lost and all that we have seen.

Before Charlie arrived, I started to have voices talk to me in my head. Clouding my thoughts for lengthy periods of time with dark themes such as *I am going to die alone*, and *I don't deserve anyone because I survived the pandemic*. I was depressed and constantly replaying all the things I could have done better in my past.

As soon as I walked into the door that morning when she had fallen down the stairs, the voices became a bit quieter and the world was a bit brighter. I think that is why I want to be with her, why I feel drawn to be with her. She grounds me just being near me.

The water started to run cold, small hot water tank, runs cold pretty fast but it is just what I needed to come back to the task at hand and get the hell out of the shower and move on with the rest of the evening.

I dry off quick, throw on some jeans and a shirt I found at Charlie's place that she said I could take. She said I could take anything, and she had said she liked this shirt and thought it would look nice on me. A crew neck knitted long-sleeve shirt, green like my eyes. And if I do say so myself, I am looking half decent. Next, deodorant, clothes for tomorrow, and whatever looked good

## Starting Again

to eat. Which is mainly some organic frozen veggies and frozen chicken. Aiming for a stir-fry.

I am out the door, hoping I hadn't taken too long, lost in my thoughts. I wonder what we will do tomorrow. I'd be happy to keep cleaning out her place and maybe walk around and explore the acreage, see how far the fencing goes.

Those million thoughts took me all the way up to the porch and before I knew it, I had opened the door and starting walking in. This isn't where I lived and didn't want to come off as too familiar, it just happened.

"Come on in," Charlie had said when she saw me frozen half in and half out of her door. Her smile made my heart feel heavy with affection. I noticed the smile first but slowly my eyes dropped down to see that she is wearing a black lace lingerie thingy top and matching lace panties, leaving extraordinarily little to the imagination, despite having seen all of it twice this morning.

I remained frozen in the doorway but not because of my intrusion, but out of shock, admiration, and all the blood had left my brain and traveled down to my cock. Instantly hard-on, the way she is standing in the doorway leading to the living room from the kitchen. Arms above her head in a V shape against the doorframe, making her beautiful breasts pop out, and one leg delicately placed slightly in front of the other. The delicate bones in her feet protruding just a little as she stood on her toes to give her a bit more height.

She is just a little too sexy for my own good. I stood for only a few moments to take her all in, from the tips of toes up all the way along her sexy slender legs, to the beginning of the lace all the way up to her face. Her hair is down and rolling down her chest like brown ski slopes.

When the moment had passed, I seemed to get my bearings back and dropped everything I am carrying, not caring at all about what it is I am carrying, stepped in all the way, closed the door, and wasted zero seconds decreasing the space between us.

"You are so sexy, you look amazing. I am going to take you upstairs and show you how sexy I think you are!" I grabbed Charlie's ass and lifted her. Naturally, her legs wrapped around my waist and I slid my hands down her smooth thighs to give her support. Our mouths connected and immediate electricity fired between us. Our lips parted to make way for our lonely tongues to caress.

"Take me right here, on the table. Show me how sexy I am here, now," Charlie whispered in my ear. I maneuvered our intertwined bodies backwards to the table, bumping into it with my body. I put her down, leaving her sitting on the edge of the table to undress myself.

As I removed the clothing I thought I looked good in not half an hour ago that were now feeling very restrictive for the current activity, Charlie is massaging her own breast with her hands, pinching her nipples like I had done this morning. Charlie's hushed moans beckoned me, but I stood back just a beat, I had never been with a woman so comfortable with pleasing herself in front of me. I wanted to remember this moment, but not for too long, there is fun to be had.

My erection had sprung out of my underwear as I had pulled them down, and noticed Charlie enjoyed watching that happen. She licked her lips as she continued to work on herself. One hand is massaging her breasts and nipples, while the other hand had gone south and she is rubbing herself through the material of the lingerie.

I approached the table and Charlie, like a predator approaching a mate. Confident strides and lust in the eyes. I maintained eye contact with Charlie the entire distance, not wanting to miss a moment of her pleasure. I wanted to be inside her badly, urgently.

"I want you inside me," Charlie demanded in a sexy, playful way.

*Starting Again*

"You read my mind again," I countered in the same sexy, playful way. Practically tearing the lingerie panties off Charlie, and with that barrier removed, I started to finger her and spread her wetness on the outside to lube her up. Charlie responded in kind with a thrust of her head backwards and displaying her breasts outward like a bird during mating season. Her legs spread in appreciation of my handiwork.

This is going to be quick and dirty, our blood is already boiling with heat. I had noticed that Charlie had shaved down to a small triangle landing patch, smooth skin exposed, exposing her clit and lips. I didn't mind her full bush this morning and don't mind the clear-cut now, as long as it is Charlie, that is my only demand.

I went in for a quick taste, a quick lick from her entry to clit and continued up to her belly button and up to her breast and to the final destination, her mouth. As I sucked in her bottom lip into my mouth, I entered her. I pulled her body closer to me, sliding her whole body closer to the edge of the table so I could go deeper. Her moan vibrated in my mouth, at the same time she gestured for me to back up and sit in one of the chairs. I did as I am told, staying inside her as I picked her up and seated us. She is straddling me now and grinding up against me.

Charlie's downstairs lips taco-ed my shaft and she slowly thrusted her hips along my erection. Charlie looked down at me, straight into my soul through my eyes. She stopped moving when the tip of my penis connected with soft, warm, and wet entrance. Rocking her hips a little forward just once to position me so that when she moved backwards I slide into her.

We both breathed a breath of pleasure, and then Charlie started to move up and down forward and backwards, and any angle in between. She is moaning, I am moaning. She is doing all the hard work and I am entranced by her beauty and her breasts, such spectacular breasts. They fit perfectly in my hands as I squeezed, rubbed, and massaged them. Her nipples were peaking out of the lace material, hard with all the good sensations.

She felt good riding me, her hands in her hair wildly grabbing handfuls. Her pace picked up, bring me closer and closer to climaxing. I could feel the explosion of passion and intense feelings with my release approaching quickly. Before the pandemic when anyone and everyone could get pregnant, condoms were a definite with my brief encounters, but since having more than half the population rendered sterile, going bareback is so wonderful. I certainly didn't last as long, slight downside.

"Come for me," Charlie almost screamed into the ceiling, "come for me, I'm coming, I'm coming." Her orgasm face and feeling her whole body tighten up on top of me and all around me sent me over the edge and the explosion came furiously with me ejaculating into her.

We both slumped in the old creaky wooden chair, breathing hard and weak from the intensity of our orgasms. I held her in my arms while she took some deep breaths and leaned with all her weight into my chest. I leaned my head on hers for a few minutes until I think we both got cold.

# Chapter 13

## Together

From that night on, actually from the morning the day before, Charlie and Everett spend almost every minute of every day together. There is so much to learn about each other, so much work to be done to keep the farms going and it is nice to do it together.

They alternated from both their homes to sleep and make food. They took down the fence between their homes and joined the animals together. And in between all the work and laughing and listening, they had heaps of sex. Didn't take much more than a brush of a hand or a seductive look to make that happen. It happened in the house, in the barn, out in a field, out in the woods; morning, noon, and night.

They fell into a lovely routine, cuddling after dinner by the fireplace, holding hands while having their morning coffee watching the sun come up over the mountains in the near distance. Days went by and neither of them ever questioned if they would or should do something together, it is just a given.

"Hey, I wanted to clear out another room at this place today after we get the morning stuff done with. Haven't really cleared out all the previous owner's stuff in the, what, almost seven months I've been here," Everett casually said as they cleared shit out of the animal stalls.

"Ya, of course, sounds like a plan. We should probably plan to go out and see if we can find a store for food and supplies. We can take the truck and get gas, too, for the gator."

Everett deeply appreciated how easy-going it is to be with Charlie. It seemed as though they were either on the same page all the time or they are extremely flexible or a little of both. "You're the best! I love you!" Everett threw his arms around Charlie's neck to give her an affectionate hug. Everett squeezed her tight to make sure she is real but mostly because he cared so wholeheartedly for her.

"Ummm, did you just tell me you loved me?" Charlie felt the same but still taken back by Everett saying it and saying it first. Charlie adored Everett and never wanted to spend a moment without him. When she is with him, life is complete. She hasn't even thought about drinking once since they met. It is probably all the therapeutic sex, but he calms the daring voices in her head that used to egg her on to drink and party.

"I did, and I do, truly love you. You make me better in every way. There are so many distinct types of love I feel for you. And don't feel like you have to say it back. Really, I am content to share how I feel, it isn't a ploy to fish for a return on that investment."

"Oh god no, I love you, too. I just wanted to make sure you meant to say it. Like not in a 'I love you, man' kind of way."

And with that they kissed, passionately standing in the middle of a cow stall. This is a tender moment being shared by two people who had survived and seen the worst things imaginable, who never thought they would be happy or find happiness. They were just chasing peace and somehow chased peace right into each other.

A few moments later, still high from the whole *I love you* moment, they were in the master bedroom of the house Everett originally moved into. Everett had been sleeping in what felt like the spare room since it didn't have any personal items in it. Everett felt uncomfortable staying in the master bedroom, a room that had memories embedded in the walls and the furniture. He imagined a family, faces provided from the pictures throughout the house, having moments, sharing their lives together. There is no telling how they passed and where and if they were together.

Holding a picture frame with a man and woman in it, having a picnic by the looks of it, smiling and looking very in love, Everett shared what is going through his mind unexpectedly, it just came out. "I feel so guilty that I lived and all my family didn't. Like this family." Everett turned the frame around to show Charlie.

"I do, too, daily. There are so many reminders everywhere."

"I struggle with the reality of just how significant this whole thing is. Why me, why not them? The whole clean-up initiative didn't help. It's been a tough three years watching people die, everywhere. Dropping dead in the grocery stores, in their cars, on the steps to the hospital. I hear voices sometimes, voices of those who I watched die, I guess. Making me question my existence. But all that seems to have changed since you arrived. I feel grounded and less guilty. Being near you quiets the voices."

Everett felt very vulnerable, open like a good book read to the middle of the story. Everett hadn't made eye contact with Charlie the whole time he talked, not intentionally, just lost in thought. Everett looked up to find Charlie with tears dropping down her cheeks. Not crying, just a few tears. Their eyes connected and Everett didn't feel ashamed for sharing a little bit of himself with Charlie. He felt safe.

"The worst was kids and babies. I don't think I've slept a solid night's sleep until I got here. I keep seeing faces in my dreams, asking me why them and to save them. So I understand. It is hard to be grateful when you feel so guilty. But we should feel grateful for this second chance. I have not been sober for exceptionally long, but I want to do better, be better with this gift. And I know it doesn't feel like a gift, not yet, but I hope someday that we both find the peace in creating a life worth a damn." Charlie spoke through the emotions stuck in her throat.

In this very moment, they may not have known it, but they were connected for life. If they nurtured this relationship right, together they would heal and overcome, and live a life with purpose.

"I guess that's why I haven't really cleared this stuff out, I feel like a thief stealing someone else's life. Home invader. Guilt just really is such a powerful thing. But I know rationally that they aren't coming back and I'm caring for the animals for them." Everett looked down at the picture frame again when he said, "I'm glad you are here."

Everett smiled, he really is glad. And you know what? Everett felt a bit lighter. There is something in knowing he isn't the only one who felt like he did, it made it okay for some reason. He isn't the bad guy in this situation, and he did deserve to continue on living.

While deep in thought, Charlie had made her way to him and is taking the frame out of his hand. She placed it back on the dresser and wrapped her arms around Everett. Together they just might figure this all out and move forward. "I got ya, buddy," Charlie whispered in Everett's ear.

The rest of the day, another sunny and cool May day, is great and productive. Charlie guided Everett in cleaning out rooms. She physically helped as well, but took care to be sensitive to how their actions made Everett feel. Asking questions and letting him dictate the task.

*Starting Again*

By the end of the day, they were exhausted and happy to have something quick to eat: a microwavable dinner of some sort and rest on the couch together. They sat in front of the fire, drinking tea and watching the flames flicker as if they were moving in slow-mo. It is quite mesmerizing, and reassuring. They sat together, in a relaxing silence, snuggling. They were in Everett's living room this evening, in his place.

There were all kinds of books and maybe later they would read, or play a game or cards, but right now they were very content. Sitting in silence watching the fire. Charlie had showered, not alone. Showers became a team effort, it is fun, sexy, and saved on hot water. Charlie had since put on her sweats and sweatshirt. Everett in a similar outfit.

"Well, I guess we have come to this point in our relationship where we are both in our sweats and it looks like neither of us care," Charlie said and had a giggle afterwards.

"We've said I love you on multiple occasions, sweats, jeans, naked, you could wear a paper bag and I would think you are beautiful," Everett countered.

"Oh, I just meant it is nice that we can be ourselves together. I don't think I could have continued to wear lingerie each night." A smirk replaced her smile.

Everett had a serious look on his face, which concerned Charlie for a few minutes. Had she said something triggering or wrong?

"I love you. I want to be with you all the time." Everett's look changed from serious to playful, tickling Charlie in the sides. Charlie is squirming and playfully fought back until she is lying on her back along the couch and Everett is on top of her.

"I love you, too, and I know this seems to be all very fast, but I don't want to miss a moment or waste a second. We got a pass from cancer and the pandemic, so we both know life is short and should be spent doing what makes you happy. You make me happy. You are like my best friend. I don't want or need you to say anything back, I just wanted you to know how I felt."

Charlie questioned if she should say something, not wanting to take away from the sincerity of what Everett had just shared, but she felt the same and in the spirit of living life to the fullest she had to say something. "I couldn't have dreamed you up if I tried." To seal the moment, Charlie kissed Everett to show that she is good with whatever, as long as it included him.

Everett reciprocated the sentiment in their kiss. They embraced for a few minutes and Everett pulled away first, he wanted to look into Charlie's eyes. "So we are exclusive?"

"Yes, outside of there being no one else, I only have eyes for you."

"Okay, just checking because I've seen the way Elvis looks at you, he wants to make a move on my girl."

"Elvis the goat? You are a funny guy."

# Chapter 14

## Together

Everett deeply cared for Charlie and found himself very fond of some of her physical features. Such as her chickenpox scars, and the beauty marks on each knee in the same place just above the kneecap. How she leaned forward when she is really laughing, and when she is so immensely amused that her laugh is silent.

Everett is fond of the fact that Charlie swears a lot and that she has a dark sense of humor. That she seems unable to be unkind even to bugs. Everett loved how sexy Charlie looked wearing his plaid shirts and, most of all, Everett appreciated that Charlie is even with her emotions. Everett isn't, at least not on the inside. On the inside it is a turbulent riptide of emotions and negativity and voices. Her steady demeanor kept his storm calm.

On this early morning as they enjoyed their coffee on the porch taking in the vast landscape, like a painting, Everett started unpacking his feelings, his feelings about Charlie, his feelings about surviving, his feelings of not wanting to waste a minute not being happy and his feelings of gratitude. While he is unpacking each box, only a little because too much would be overwhelming and then he would be stuck with being unable to decide whether or not to keep going or put them away, he had a thought.

Everett had kept his hair long because he had lost it during his treatment for cancer. Before, it had symbolized to him his victory. When he touched his hair or saw his hair it reminded him of being healthy and cancer-free. It reminded him of when he was going through treatment, how sick he had become and weak. So he associated the feeling of weakness with short hair. But now something is different, those feelings didn't automatically pop up for him. It is quite striking to Everett the lack of something that had been part of him for the last, what, four years, the feeling of not wanting to be weak.

Everett must have been touching his hair because Charlie had asked him what he is thinking about. "Nothing, really, just thinking about what we are going to do today."

"Well, okay then. It's another beautiful day and we have work to do, Mr. Peterson!" And with that Charlie is up and ready for the day.

Everett had started a lot of the veggie seedlings back in March and they were going to test out the greenhouse by planting them outside directly. They were varieties; cauliflower, broccoli, Brussels sprouts, kale and turnips, that were said to be able to thrive in the cooler earlier months, so fingers crossed that the last frost had already happened. They had planned to direct sow as well, as a test. Lots of gardening to do!

The sun rose and shared the heat from its rays with the land and all who lived on it. The day passed with chores and joking and chatting. The sun is up longer now, really felt like summer is around the corner. The mood is chipper and light, and lots of work got done. But now tummies grumbled with hunger, which is their flag that it is around five p.m. They had missed lunch so it is definitely time to clean up and make dinner.

Everett and Charlie often showered at the same time, and if not in the same shower, in their respective homes. Today is no different and they were showering in their own homes. There is always a deep passionate kiss and a "hurry back" exchanged before they go separate ways. Everything is very uncomplicated when it came to the two of them as a couple.

Everett, standing naked fresh from the shower in front of the mirror, reliving his own internal conversation with himself from this morning. His hair, even now looking at it, didn't bring him the same feelings of strength, nor is it any longer a symbol of strength. Before he knew it he had scissors in his hands, as if being controlled by a separate being. And he started cutting away with no thought of what the desired finished look would be.

Once he is done with his hair, he did add style to it not just a lob job or bowl cut, he just kept going and shaved his beard while he is on a roll. His skin is so sensitive and burned like holy hell. As if the spirit of a possessed person had left the body, Everett refocused into the present, looking at the reflection. The face looking back is not one he had seen in a long time and at the same time is older and different. He liked who is looking back, and Everett is thinking not only about the physical appearance but how he felt about himself inside.

Everett dressed, leaving this hairy mess on the floor to be dealt with later, and made his way back to Charlie. While he crossed the distance between the two houses, Everett noticed smoke from the chimney, which meant Charlie had started a fire and he could smell bread cooking. How long had he been gone? he wondered.

He paused for a moment at the door before going in. He looked through the glass panes of the door and watched Charlie putter around the kitchen. She is so beautiful, her hair, her movements, her carefree aura. And she is in one of his plaid shirts again, made his engines fire up just thinking of her slender body naked inside his shirt.

He opened the door and stepped inside. Charlie turned to look at him with a smile on her face to say something, a sentenced queued up on her lips. But no words came out, she looked shocked and her mouth fell open as a result. Everett worried that she may not like the fresh look, but waited for her to say something.

"Oh, my gawd, you look amazing! When, how, why. Look at your face, oh my god look at your hair! It's so short, when did you do this all? Is that why it took you so long to get cleaned up and head back here? I thought you changed your mind or you fell in a well." Charlie brought her hands up to her face to cover her mouth in sheer shock. "I love it so much; you are so handsome. You were handsome before but now I can see your face, all of your face. And look at your hair, I can't get over it. You did this?"

Charlie, for the first time in the last five minutes, started to walk towards Everett. Navigating around the table that had been in between them, and when she is inches from him, stroked his hair in disbelief and amazement.

Everett felt relief that Charlie liked it, the act is symbolic to him, but he still wanted her to find him attractive. They were never stuck with each other, either could walk away and start new somewhere else. That is not at all what he wanted but their relationship is still so new and it started so hot right out of the gate. But she genuinely seemed to like it and Everett liked that she is playing in his hair right now.

"I did do it; first time I've ever cut my own hair. You do like it? You can be honest."

"I love it, both styles look amazing on you. I just like that I can see more of you, and I can touch more of you, and I can kiss more of you, and . . ." Charlie's words trailed off as she leaned closer to place her face a paper-width from his. Charlie stopped just for a brief moment to look him in his green eyes and then covered the rest of the distance to kiss him. Oh, how different it is to kiss him without his mustache and beard tickling her lips.

She started kissing him gently, but the excitement of kissing someone who looked like a different man than she had kissed about an hour ago turned her pressure and depth of her kisses to something filled with desire. Their lips parted to let their tongues search and feel the other's.

Charlie stepped into Everett, like the air being sucked out of a bag, their bodies collapsed into each other. As one body they collapsed to the floor with Everett on top. Charlie raised her bare legs up and apart to let Everett get direct contact with her body.

Everett ran a hand from her ankle along her smooths leg, up to the knee, rounded the corner to her thigh like a race car driving a track. When he made it to her hip he noticed that she isn't wearing any underwear, sparking hormones to fire throughout his body and signaling blood to rush to his penis, giving him a raging erection.

His hands kept exploring up her ribs and Charlie moaned when he made it to her breasts. Everett groaned in response to her moan and at being amazed once again with the shape and feel of the breast in his hand. Her hard nipple is a sign that she is aroused and Everett is equally aroused by her arousal. Her breast felt a bit fuller than last time they had made love and wondered if she is going to start her period soon. Everett is an evolved man, periods did not scare him, nor did talking about it or entertaining the thought of making love during it. His girlfriend before the pandemic had taught him the ins and outs.

Charlie's skin is so soft, so inviting to touch, all over her body. Charlie responded more vibrantly to his touch, he wondered if it is because he cut his hair and shaved. Didn't know, didn't care. This is the now and this is fantastic.

Something primal came over Everett in that second, he parted from Charlie, straddling her. He ripped open her shirt, sending the buttons flying in every other direction, sliding along the floor to all corners of the kitchen. Charlie's eyes widened, turned on by the act and shocked simultaneously.

Charlie had her whole front fully exposed as she had no undergarments under the shirt. She is fully naked and open. Everett shimmied back off her legs and raised them in the air until her butt is pointed northeast. Everett buried his face in the center of her V-shaped position, feeling her skin against his freshly shaved face is exciting. More of him to feel more of her. He stiffened his tongue and entered her with it, pushing it in and out.

From there he licked the center part of her lips from opening to clit, sucking in her clit once he is there. Charlie moaned and squirmed, Everett is pleased with the sound he made come out of Charlie. Everett is a hundred percent focused on the task at hand that he hadn't noticed that Charlie's moans became more of pain than pleasure. Or when her hand that was playfully squeezing his hair and massaging his scalp as he gave her oral sex, has now turned a bit more pulling than squeezing. What did bring him back to earth is when Charlie said the word "Ouch!"

"What's wrong, am I hurting you?" Everett immediately stopped what he is doing and looked up to Charlie's face for a sign of what caused her pain.

"Something is digging into my back. I think I'm bleeding."

They had not noticed that the kitchen throw rug had moved a bit in their movements along the floor. The throw rug had never moved before and you could see it lived in that same spot for many years as it had protected the floor from sun and wear and tear.

Charlie wiggled out from being bent around like a pretzel and into a position more in line with getting up, to get a better look at what had attacked her. As they both stood and looked down to the approximate place Charlie's back had made contact with the floor, they noticed that there is a metal latch peaking from under the carpet.

## *Starting Again*

Everett is the first to lean down to throw the carpet out of the way to expose a trapdoor in the floor. All that they could see is the outline of the square door and the latch. Looking at each other silently and simultaneously, their eyes spoke and understood that they both wanted to open the door to see what is inside.

During their time together, and even before when Everett had first arrived, when exploring the houses they had both found many books on gardening, living like in the olden days, living off-grid, homesteading with no modern techniques or tools, those sorts of books. Charlie had read one during one of their quiet evenings together about having cold storage for root veggies to keep them edible longer into the winter season. Having the natural coolness of the deep earth keep the veggies and canned, jarred goods cold and preserved longer. Charlie had immediately thought they had discovered a cold cellar.

Everett unlatched the door and lifted it open, a cool breeze escaped from its prison and chilled both of them to the bone. It is definitely cold down there and almost as cold as a freezer. It is also very dark and neither of them could see anything. Charlie went to get a flashlight from on top of the fridge while Everett held the door.

Not realizing he is still holding it when he could lay it down on the floor opposite to where he had just opened it from, he laid it down as Charlie got the flashlight. Charlie shone the light to expose a set of wooden stairs leading further into darkness. Charlie shivered from the coolness and the creepiness, but decided to forge on, if there were any fresh vegetables down there or organic preserves, she is willing to risk the monsters living in the dark.

Without any hesitation, Charlie started making her way down into the dungeon. Everett grabbed her arm and handed her the shirt he had torn off her body not moments ago. "You're as naked as the day you were born. Want to put some clothes on before heading down into the dark, creepy hole in the kitchen?" Not so much a question as it is a reminder of the state she is in.

"Oh, ya, good idea!" She slipped on the shirt and retrieved some pants from the laundry room off the kitchen, bringing a pair of boots for each of them. Even faced with fear and curiosity, Charlie is still taken aback at how handsome Everett is all cleaned up. It would take her a while to get used to it, not in a bad way, just in a habit kind of way.

Dressed and flashlight in hand, Charlie once again started making her way down the stairs. Everett is impressed by her bravery or whatever Charlie is displaying right now, and to be honest, deep down he didn't want to go in the hole that led to the devil's bedroom. But once Charlie started the charge with no hesitation, he felt he had no options.

So away they went down the stairs, there isn't more than about seven steps, and then they hit a dirt floor. There is just enough space to stand up, well for Charlie, Everett had to duck a little. The whole room is dirt and quite vast, the ray of the light didn't make it to each wall standing at the base of the stairs.

From where they stood, it did look like a cold storage room: there were many shelves lining the walls filled with preserves and boxes presumably holding veggies, or *hopefully* is a better word. Charlie rushed over to the shelves, paying attention to nothing else, so excited about the prospect of eating something fresh-ish.

"Oh, Everett, there are carrots and squash and beets, and they feel and look like they are still good. Must have been their last crop. Oh, come see them!" Charlie motioned with a free hand and waved him over to her with her face still buried in the wooden box. It took a few minutes for Charlie to register that Everett is not making his way over, so she tore her eyes from the food to look at him to see what the delay is.

Everett had a look on his face that she could only describe as having just seen a ghost. His face is pale and his eyes wide. He held his flashlight pointed to the wall past where she is standing. She followed his gaze all the way behind her to the right of her, to the wall at the far end of the storage room. Where she saw four human bodies sitting on the floor slumped over each other. Not moving, not breathing.

Everett had recognized them all as the previous owners of both their houses. The pictures that had been in the houses were imprinted in his memory. Neither of them screamed, the bodies didn't smell and had only decomposed a little. They were frozen solid and well-preserved like the non-human items stored down here.

Charlie is the first to notice that a gun lies next to one of the bodies, and with closer inspection they all had gunshot holes in their heads. There is blood splatter like art up and along the wall behind them. Everett knelt down next to the closest body, the husband who lived in his house who is next to his wife, and beside her is the wife and then the husband of Charlie's house. They were in almost a circle, sitting on the floor.

There are congealed droplets of blood around the entry wound of three of them and they all lacked a back of the head. They had definitely died by a gunshot to the head. But why come down here to die? And the husband from Everett's house who is next to the gun, clearly had shot himself, as his didn't have a entry wound, which means he had the gun in his mouth.

"This is all very strange. Maybe they didn't want the animals to eat them and get sick, why else come down here to die?" Charlie broke the silence as she moved next to Everett. Her statement is as if she is finishing a sentence out loud that she had started inside her head.

"It is, really. I recognize them all. Husband and wife who lived at my place and husband and wife who lived here." Everett pointed to them as he described them so Charlie could see who he is talking about. "I recognize them from the photos, in the frames from the master bedrooms."

"There isn't a lot known about the virus when it first started spreading, there had been reports of it infecting animals in the early days," Charlie offered.

"Ya, true, lots of different theories at the beginning. But these bodies don't look like they ended their lives years ago, they look like months ago. I've seen death in all stages and forms as part of the navy, and I would say they have been dead about six to eight months."

"But wouldn't the cold slow down decomposition?" Charlie pondered out loud.

"Again, ya, maybe, probably. I don't really know, a bit outside my expertise. Aren't you freaked out by the dead bodies?"

"Not really. The great clean-up cleared me of any fear or disgust with dead bodies. Saw my fair share of all sorts of horrors."

Everett had accepted that answer; it is better than finding out she is a serial killer and is unphased by the dead bodies because she used to have a collection of her own. "I guess we will have to bury them or burn them tomorrow. Too late to move them now. We can sleep at my place tonight and deal with it in the morning. You okay with that?" Everett offered.

"Not sure I'd use the word *okay* but it does seem like the most logical plan of action. I'll go grab some of my things and we can head over. I'm looking for creepy underground storage things at your place just in case. Have you ever seen the movie *The Road*? This is very much like that, but they were keeping live humans in one of these things as food." Charlie couldn't help making a freaked-out face at the memory of the movie.

"You are a strange and odd and fabulous human being Charlie Wolfe; keeping things interesting." Everett smiled and reached out to take Charlie's hand, which she accepted and allowed Everett to lead her up the stairs. They closed the trapdoor and moved the

*Starting Again*

table on top of the door, just in case, you know, to keep the dead bodies down there and the alive things up here.

# Chapter 15

## Together

They did as they had decided earlier, they gathered up some supplies and headed over to Everett's place.

Spent the rest of the evening and night eating and sitting in silence, processing what they had found. It is extra odd now having the deceased owners in a cellar next door. Moving into a home that you know was not vacated for happy reasons is odd on its own, but them not gone and not alive is very odd.

Their discovery had put a permanent halt on this evening's sexy times, and they needed to make a big fire to warm their chilled bones. The hot shower had not done the trick for either of them. They didn't often watch movies, but tonight felt like as good of a time as any to distract them, finding a comedy they both enjoyed: *Ferris Bueller's Day Off*.

Neither really watched the movie, both were preoccupied with the bodies and their dreaded task tomorrow morning. Everett's mind, having come from a structured employment such as the navy, also went in the direction of how long will it last that no one is paying for electricity, in the areas that still had some. Before all the bills and taxes returned. Having to pay for food. He wondered if the previous owners had the same thought, which is why they had decided to run this hobby farm originally.

Charlie, on the other hand, is thinking how far away and claustrophobic she felt at this very moment. An odd feeling to be in such a wide-open space but she felt trapped in the vastness of the space. How long would it take to find other people, how far would they have to drive. She missed her comforts and familiarities of her previous home. Especially having to deal with the dead bodies in the floor freezer.

Charlie and Everett sat close to one another for the entire movie, not really having watched the movie but the closeness of the other person is of comfort. They both appreciated having the other there, they both couldn't imagine going through this alone.

After the movie is done, Charlie stood up and instantly felt nauseous. A little more than nauseous, she is actually going to throw up. It is so sudden that she stood there a bit longer than she should have in puzzlement, so she barely made it to the bathroom. Everett isn't far behind her offering support and whatever she needed.

All her dinner made a reappearance in a pureed state, all of it so very violently. She wiped her mouth with toilet paper and flushed the toilet. Being sick in front of others is not her favorite thing, and she is immediately uncomfortable that Everett, who is so kindly holding her hair, is in the room with her and witnessing this unexpected event. Charlie attempted to clean up and started moving around to distract Everett from asking any questions and to get both of them out of the bathroom as soon as she could. Charlie started brushing her teeth and walked out of the bathroom in hopes that Everett would follow her, but he didn't, he waited until she came back.

## Starting Again

Charlie peeked around the edge of the doorframe, toothbrush shoved to one side of her mouth. Everett is looking at her with a question mark visible on his face. Charlie is unsure if he is wondering why she threw up or why she reacted the way she did afterwards.

"Are you okay?"

"Yes, I think so. Not sure why I was sick. I feel fine now." Charlie put on her most convincing face.

"Do you remember the last time you had a tetanus shot, is your jaw getting stiff?" Everett asked, assessing the symptoms to come to the most logical conclusion, as he had done a million times before as a medic.

"Oh no, jaw feels fine, and I couldn't even begin to remember if and when I had my last tetanus shot."

"Can I see your back? I'll take a look at the scratch the latch made again. Don't want you getting any infections or some sort of poisoning."

Charlie is relieved that the question mark on Everett's face is not as to why she acted as she did after throwing up and hopefully this will be the only time that he will ever see that. Charlie lifted her sweater to expose her wound, small as it is. Everett examined it again and it looked okay, not hot to the touch or red around the edges. He checked Charlie for any signs of a fever. All clear, but he did decide to put some more antiseptic on it and cover it up with a new gauze and tape.

"Are you sure you are okay? What we saw earlier was heavy and gross, you think maybe you are just releasing those feelings now and it made you sick?" Everett furrowed his eyebrows in concern.

"Maybe. It didn't bother me then nor does it bother me now. I mean, the actual dead body part. Knowing them is a different feeling altogether. I truly feel much better, I think I'm fine."

Charlie had toothpaste in her mouth as she spoke and it was getting spicy, she needed to spit and rinse out the residue. She had successfully held it all in her mouth while talking but her mouth is now starting to burn from the mint and drool in response. As she spits the toothpaste into the sink, in the corner of her eye she notices all of Everett's hair on the floor from when he must have cut it. Everett, who notices Charlie looking at the hair on the ground, is now himself uncomfortable that he forgot to clean up his mess. "I wasn't expecting us to be here tonight. I'll clean that up after I get you a glass of water."

The weather outside had turned and this is the first time Charlie heard rain hit the roof and the wind howl. It had been a crazy evening and all of a sudden she is wiped out. "I'm exhausted, I think I'm going to go to bed. If you want to stay up, please do, but I can barely keep my eyes open."

Everett is filling the glass that he keeps in the bedroom up with water for Charlie. "No, I'll come with you, keep an eye on you!" Everett replied and as he is walking by her he slapped her butt in a loving gesture. Sex is completely off the table tonight, they weren't savages, but this is more of a slap of comfort in the relationship. A sign that they were a couple and even though they had verbally confirmed that they were exclusive, this is an outward demonstration to echo that commitment.

Charlie smiled and slapped his ass in return, they were being playful, which is an enjoyable way to end this day. Charlie giggled as she ran away to hide in the bedroom, Everett chased her and gave her loving kisses when he caught her. They embraced, molding their bodies together as they had done earlier, but this time they peeled apart and went to bed.

# Chapter 16

## Charlie

I can't remember why I came to the barn, but I'm standing at the door trying to really think. As I am aging I am acutely aware that my memory is not what it once was. I often find myself in a room wondering why I am there. I am retracing my steps mentally backwards to see if I can spark that memory as to why I am here. As I think, I am watching the goats and chickens being goats and chickens. The cows are out in the fields so the barn is otherwise quiet and still.

I can feel the sun's heat warming up my back, it feels wonderful. It is a cool morning and the inside of the barn is cool on my front. So the heat feels perfect. I have a quick thought as to where Everett is, maybe he remembers why I am here. Maybe he asked me to come to the barn to get him something. No matter, the heat feels great so I am going to stand here just a few moments longer. I look at all the tools to see if that is why I am here and nothing jumps to mind. So I decide to leave. As I start turning my body to head back to the house, a movement at the back corner of the barn catches my eye.

I turn back and there is nothing there. I look to my left, the goats and chickens are where they were when I last looked at them. Must have been a strand of hair falling in my peripheral vision. It was fast, so couldn't have been one of the animals. Long hair struggles are real, people!

Pleased with my deduction, I turn again to leave and again I see a shadow move quickly in the same place. Well, what the fuck is going on? I pull my hair back and tie it up with an elastic I carry on my wrist for emergencies such as this. Already a bit irritated with myself for forgetting why I am here, I am becoming even more irritated that I am now seeing things.

I enter the barn and maneuver around the stalls and beams and piles of hay in the direction of where I saw movement. There is a stall for baby cows in the back corner a bit closed off and isolated, scary to think babies would be put there away from their mothers. I won't do that; families will stay together at this farm.

I duck down and I go under a beam blocking me horizontally, and as I stand up a nail sticking out nicks me in the back. *Ouch!* I instinctively reach a hand to the sore spot to ease a bit of the pain as I rub the area with my frozen fingers. The barn is cold and there is no heat from the sun anymore, I am suddenly chilled and my body shivers in the hope to warm me up a bit.

I hear a noise from the isolated stall that makes the hair on my arms and neck stand up, straight up as if they are trying to leave this world without me. What is that? Did it sound like an animal or is it the barn's structure just shifting and settling with age? The adrenaline my body injected into my bloodstream is making my heart beat faster. It is strange because usually you start to overheat when your heart is beating this fast but I'm still freezing.

"Come on, get out of there, whatever you are. Don't be jumping out at me, barn owl or cat or goat. That wouldn't be very nice!"

*Starting Again*

A louder sound answers my plea, but not in a comforting way. It almost sounds like a deep, throaty moan. Then there is a shuffling sound as if something is stuck and trying to scurry away. I pause for a moment and all I hear is my heartbeat, trying to thrash its way out of my rib cage. No sound at all, not even the chickens or goats I saw before.

Darkness falls over the barn like thick black paint is being poured over the roof, the light from the windows starts fading as if curtains are being pulled down. I look out the window only to understand I can't see anything anymore except pitch-black. My skin crawls, I don't like this. I don't understand this. I need to find Everett, I need to leave the barn.

My brain is screaming but I can't understand what it is saying. I'm trying to understand what is going on outside. I hear screaming, a high-pitched scream. That's not coming from inside me, it is coming from outside of me. I look in the direction of the screaming, in the direction of the isolated stall.

There is a human standing where no human had been standing before. Hunched a little, almost drooping. I don't see well in the dark, my eyes are still adjusting, but I can see a shape and it is a person. And that person is screeching. I cover my ears to protect my eardrums, it is so loud. Why is it so loud?

I open my mouth to talk but no words come out, not a sound. I go to let out a scream myself, hopefully Everett will hear me, but . . . nothing. I am soundless and feel helpless. This person and I are facing each other and screaming in each other's direction except they are actually screaming, but I'm only making the motions of screaming. My legs are heavy, I can move but it is very cumbersome. I look down at my legs to see if they are stuck in mud or tar, but they are free.

I do notice that I have blood on my thighs and I follow the trail up to my crotch. I am bleeding heavily, and I start having cramps but not cramps I'm used to, these are way worse. It feels like I am miscarrying but I am not with child and have never been with child or miscarried. The blood keeps flowing, flowing down my leg and over my boots. "Someone help me," I scream without a sound.

The other person in the corner stops screaming, the quietness is deafening. I turn my gaze back in that direction to an empty space. There is no one there. I start looking side to side, searching for them, and then the chill returns, but only against my back. I feel as if I am lying down on a frozen pond with no shirt on.

That's when the moaning starts and it is coming from behind me. A gurgled moan. It felt close, right in my ear, I could almost feel their breath against my exposed neck. I am instantly terrified but I feel compelled to turn around and face whatever is behind me. I slowly turn, my body is shaking so bad I feel like I am convulsing, that my bones will snap from the intensity of my shaking. I take that last step to the left to make the full 90-degree turn and there I am facing the husband, the one who owned Everett's house, the guy from the cold storage cellar.

He is standing there in front of me with only a few inches between us. I can feel the cold coming from his body. I suddenly realize that there is light coming from somewhere because I can see the blue hue of his skin, the milky color that his eyes have become, how sunken his eye sockets are. He is not screaming anymore, but his mouth gaping open and the blood that is running down my leg is now oozing from his mouth, over his stained teeth and blue lips. It is dark, the blood, almost black like roofing tar.

I can't move, I can't scream, and no one is coming to help me. I can't stop staring at his decaying features. I can feel he wants to hurt me, to kill me. I close my eyes and wish him away. This can't be real, he is dead in the ground, he can't be here. Please be gone, please be gone, please be gone. The moaning has stopped, I didn't hear any motions but it is quiet again. I open my eyes and he's still

*Starting Again*

there, but he is reaching for me, his bony gray-skinned hand is reaching for me.

He grabs my arm and starts pulling me to him, like bringing me into his lair. He stretches his mouth to its fullest capacity, to its limits. The skin at the corners of his mouth are see-through like wet rice paper. As I get closer I can smell the rotting flesh stench coming from his mouth. I gag so bad, I think I'm going to throw up. I try screaming again and I finally let out a scream and I put all of my lung power into it.

## Chapter 17

## Together

"Charlie, Charlie, Charlie, wake up. You are having a bad dream. Babe, wake up." Everett is gently shaking Charlie by the arm with his hand. "Baby, wake up, it is just a dream."

Charlie wakes up with a start. "I'm going to throw up again!" She throws the blanket off of her in a mad rush for the bathroom. It is dark but her eyes have adjusted so she can safely make it to the toilet. She doesn't even turn on the light, there is no time. And just making it to dry-heave a couple times before bile burns its way from her stomach to out of her mouth.

This time she doesn't quickly gather herself and clean up, she is sweating, exhausted, and on the verge of crying. Mostly from the nightmare, but a little for how much she hates throwing up. She is kneeling in front of the toilet as one does when puking, and without a care in this very moment. She has her head propped up against the edge of the bowl. The coolness feels nice against her hot, sweaty forehead.

Her top is soaked through, from the dream and throwing up, and just seconds before she had felt like she was burning to death, but now she is shivering. Everett is back to his post as hair holder and back rubber. He doesn't mind the sweat, he is genuinely concerned now that Charlie might have an infection. There is a first aid kit somewhere in the kitchen, he has seen it. Where is it? He has walked by it a million times, why can't he remember where it is? "Stay here. I'm going to look for something in the kitchen, I'll be right back."

Charlie isn't going anywhere, despite feeling a million times better. She is happy right where she is. Everett had hurriedly made it down the hallway to the kitchen. He had to get used to two different layouts when it comes to the homes. Charlie's place is two stories and this place is a rancher. He sometimes went the wrong way when he wasn't paying attention. Now in the kitchen he stood in the doorway pondering where the first aid kit could be. Where had he seen it? It feels like it should be somewhere obvious.

Realizing he is standing in the dark, turning on the light might be a promising idea, and so it is. Everett flicked on the light to the kitchen, which blinded him for a half minute, but he eventually adjusted. Almost immediately, like a flash went off in his mind, in his memories, he remembered where the kit is. He retrieved it from a cupboard because, yes, that is the best place for it, and ran back to Charlie.

She had not moved but the color had returned to her face and she is no longer leaning on the toilet. Everett took out the thermometer from the kit and did the gestures that all moms did to their kids, like open your mouth and leave it under your tongue. Charlie obliged weakly and kept the thermometer secured under her tongue with her mouth closed. She did, however, make eye contact with Everett and held it with her Bambi eyes.

## Starting Again

The device made a signal that it had a reading to share. Everett removed it and brought it into his view. "No fever, phew." Everett looked at Charlie and noticed her looking at him in a peculiar way. "What, why are you looking at me that way? Are you okay? Are you going to puke again?"

"Did you call me *babe*?" Charlie asked with zero emotions on her face.

"What?" Everett looked confused for a second, throwing him deep into thought. He had his focus on figuring out why Charlie kept throwing up, not what he called her. Once he recentered he realized he had called her *babe* and *baby* without even thinking about it. He is very aware that his cheeks are flushed, and he didn't know why he is embarrassed or maybe he is just feeling shy. He had only been in one meaningful relationship before, but she had left him when he got sick. Plus being in the navy you don't really have the time to invest in a relationship.

"It's okay, I really liked it and want you to keep calling me that. It is just the first time and I wanted to make sure I heard right since I was preoccupied with throwing up. Which, by the way, is my least favorite thing to do and my absolute least favorite thing to do in front of others. Especially a sexy hot man who calls me babe." Charlie forced a smile because she really did like him giving her a pet name, it's just that dream and being sick again has her feeling out of sorts.

"I did call you that and I'm glad you liked it because I liked calling you that. I hadn't intended to, and I guess if I am going to take it out for a test run might as well be when you are distracted and puking." Everett gave a little laugh at his own joke. "How are you feeling now? Do you want to set up camp closer to the bathroom?"

"No, I think I'm okay. I was having a horrible nightmare and I think with the day's events that I worked up my stomach. Let's hope that that is it and we can both sleep the next few hours before the sun comes up."

"Listen, I can get up and feed the animals alone this morning, you sleep in, and we will tackle our other chores either later or the next day. It is freezing down there so we can take a day before we bury them."

Everett is helping Charlie off the ground when she summoned all her might to look up at him. "Noooo, we burn the bodies. No burying, no giving them a chance to resurrect!" She squeezed his arm like the monster in her dreams had done to her arm, hard.

"Oh, oh, okay. We can absolutely do that. Can you maybe tell me why you look like you just saw a ghost?" Charlie's eyes looked feverish, and she had gone pale again. Without any warning to her or Everett she began to cry, taking Everett by surprise. He, without hesitation, wrapped his arms around her and held her tight and let her sob into his chest. It is not a long cry, just a burst of feelings. When she finally seems to be settling down a bit, he picked her up off her feet and carried her in his arms to the bed. Placing her down with care.

"I think you should sleep in and take a day to yourself. Relax and forget all about any chores or dead bodies or anything like that. I will handle it all and help you with whatever you need. Do you want a tea right now, something warm to hold?"

"I'm sorry I don't know what happened there. I don't usually cry; it is not a normal thing for me. Not that there is anything wrong with crying, just not used to it. I dreamt that the guy who shot the three others was in the barn, dead but alive. Frozen and oozing with blood. Well, I was oozing with blood, too, and I couldn't move or get away. We burn the bodies!"

"You got it, burn the bodies, no arguments from me. And don't apologize for crying, it happens to the best of us. Now do you want tea, madame?"

"Yes, please that would be great, if there is any chamomile."

## Starting Again

Everett moved to get up, but Charlie lunged at him, and squeezed him tight in a hug. He held her for a few minutes, and finally he kissed the top of her head and told her he would be right back with the tea. He added before he left that they could keep hugging when he came back.

When Everett returned with the tea, Charlie is fast asleep in bed, snuggled up in the blankets and everything. Everett is happy she had fallen asleep and he would do his best not to wake her up now or in the morning. Let her rest. He really hoped she didn't have a stomach flu. If it is, the task of disposing of the bodies would become more challenging on his own. He would figure it out. He got into bed and the minute his body is fully in and covered, Charlie curled up right next to him inching her way under his arm to lay her head on his chest. And that is the way they stayed for the rest of their sleep together.

# Chapter 18

## Everett

When I woke up, purely out of habit, at five a.m., I one hundred and ten percent did not want to move. Knowing the animals needed to be fed got me moving but it is sprinkled with resistance. Charlie is dead to the world and that is exactly as I wanted to leave her this morning. Comfy and getting the rest she needed.

I got up quietly and tiptoed around to get dressed, had a quick breakfast, had some black power water better known as coffee and headed out the door. It is raining this morning, which is good for the seeds and the garden, and less work for us to water as an added bonus. Looking at the amount of feed for the animals, we might have to make our first trip out to get supplies soon. Grab some food and necessities at the same time. I am trying to make a mental list of everything we should get, but it's a hard lesson learned since my memory isn't my best friend at the best of times, so I wandered to the workshop where I knew there is paper and a pen.

After writing the list, I busied myself feeding the animals and milking the cows and letting my mind wander as I worked along. I thought a lot about Charlie and how attached I felt to her. I thought about the dead bodies and what would explain their final actions and the location they chose to do that. I thought about how we were going to move them, or more specifically, how I am going to move them. We'd need a tractor to carry them far enough away from the house to be burnt.

Thinking about that made me think about Charlie's dream. She is probably having that dream and feeling sick from the emotions of the day. I hadn't really thought about how I felt, but I am good. It is incredibly sad and will make forgetting about it difficult. Not sure how long it would be before I slept in Charlie's house. I don't think Charlie would put up a big fight for us to sleep there anytime soon.

I collected eggs, the hens were much happier in the June weather and producing way more eggs. Despite today's rain it is still fairly warm. The humidity will still make the need for a fire but it is uplifting to feel like summer is here. Thinking back, it has felt like Charlie has been here for more than just a month and a bit. Simply by how much I care for her and want to be with her all the time.

Lost in thought, I also remember I forgot to clean my hair clippings up again and would have to try really hard to remember today. It is close to noon now and will have to go in soon to eat, I am hungry, but I don't want to wake up Charlie if she is still sleeping. But on the other hand, I should check on her and see how she is doing. *Maybe she doesn't want me to check in on her, maybe she doesn't want me at all. I'm forgetful and lazy, who wants that in a partner?* the negative voice said inside my ears. This hasn't happened in a while, maybe we are both in shock and dealing in separate ways.

*Starting Again*

As if running away from a bully, I ran quickly to the house to escape the voice. Leaving it behind to pick on someone else. When I got to the door I peeked inside to see if I could see her moving about the house. I didn't see anyone but thought she could be awake in bed, and I hoped to hell she isn't puking again. The last thought made me panic a little and hastily opened the door and called out her name. Thankfully, a voice replied to me, it is Charlie's, not one in my head, from the bedroom.

"Hey, how are you doing?" I called back as I took my wet jacket off and removed my muddy boots, then walked to the bedroom where Charlie was as I waited for an answer.

"I'm good, I feel much better. Thank you for letting me get some rest. I'm starving though, want to have lunch together?"

"Sure, I'll make it. What are you in the mood for? Grilled cheese with some of that bread you made and the fake cheese slices?"

"YES, that would be perfect! You are my savior, I love you." Saying I love you is still new for us, and we didn't say it all the time but I had taken care of her and nursed her when she felt sick, so it didn't feel out of place.

"No problem, babe, anything to keep you feeling better." I emphasized the *babe* part, I knew she enjoyed hearing it and I equally enjoyed saying it. I set out to prepare lunch for us while Charlie read in the living room by the window.

"Hey, have you realized that you have been here for a month and a bit already? I was thinking of that this morning while doing stuff around the farms. Feels like time is flying, feels like yesterday I was going to that door over there and found the most beautiful woman sprawled out on the floor!" I had a gigantic smile plastered on my face.

"You are feeling cheeky this afternoon! You are going the right way for a smacked bottom!"

"Oh, are we going to try some S&M later on?" I teased back and laughed lightly. Charlie is in a playful mood as well and

*111*

started giggling. Having made her way from the living room to the kitchen, she had now been standing watching me make the grilled cheese sandwiches for a few seconds. So she grabbed one of the dish towels, spun it tight, and laid a good old snap on my behind. It landed with the sound of lightening.

"How is that? Something you want more of?"

"Ouch, holy shit, that is a good hit! That is going to leave a mark." I am rubbing his sore cheek and seeking out my own towel to serve revenge, revenge for the bruised butt cheek. Charlie is laughing from the belly, quite pleased with herself and preparing to defend herself at the same time.

We stood facing each other, towels in hand, circling the round kitchen table anticipating the other's attack. We flicked their dish towels across the table just missing the other a few times, laughing and delighted in the moment we were sharing. But Charlie's stomach had gone from feeling frisky to feeling pukey again. Her hand shot up to her mouth, towel and all, but it is too late. Vomit had breached the lip barricade and vomit fired out all over the table and me.

There isn't much, to be fair, a couple of crackers and mostly water. But nonetheless, it clear to me that Charlie was mortified. Could this get any worse for her? Charlie began cleaning up the mess quickly with the towel in her hand. "Oh my god. I'm so sorry, let me get that. I am mortified. I don't know what is wrong with me. Maybe I am just hungry, I don't know."

"Don't worry about it, the animals have done far worse to me!" I said, telling the truth but spreading it on thick to be kind as well. I didn't want Charlie feeling mortified, it happens. "Having been on a navy boat for most of my twenties and thirties, sailors have expelled far more and way more disgusting stuff, trust me. You are good, I promise. Let me get that. What luck we had both having towels in hand," I joked, hoping to lighten the mood. Which seemed to work a bit. Charlie did give a microscopic smile as she busied herself with cleaning up her mess.

I ran down the hallway quickly to change my clothes, leaving Charlie in the kitchen, and bellowed from there, "We should really do a run into a town or store to pick up supplies. I have a list started I'll bring it out, it is in my jean pocket here. If you think of anything we need to pick up."

"Everett, I think we need to get a pregnancy test, we should put one of those on the list."

# Chapter 19

# Together

Everett stopped mid-pull of the sweater over his head. He isn't sure that he heard that right. "Did you say pregnancy test?"

"Yes," Charlie was quick to reply. Everett's brain just stopped functioning entirely. Just white, no thoughts or feelings, just nothing.

Meanwhile, Charlie, who is in the kitchen alone, couldn't stop her brain from going down every single rabbit hole. Is she overthinking it, is she jumping the gun, is her math accurate, had she been here a whole month and gone without a period? They had sex every day, at least once a day, since she met him, and she had been here for over a month. She arrived May 2 and it was now June 11. Sex every day plus no period must equal pregnant. But how? The vaccine had rendered almost all the survivors sterile, as far as Charlie knew. There are no known cases of pregnancy or giving birth to a post-pandemic baby.

Everett eventually rebooted long enough to finish putting on his shirt and start inching his way to the doorway, peering around the corner to see if he could see Charlie down the hall in the kitchen. And he could. She is sitting at the table looking like she is solving the earth's problem for gas emissions. He didn't want to stay in the bedroom forever but he is sort of numb and lost.

Charlie looked up long enough to catch Everett in the corner of her eye staring down the hall at her. "I could be wrong, but I haven't had my period since I've been here, right? Could that be why I'm sick all of a sudden?"

Everett shook his head in the no motion, she isn't wrong, no period that he had seen. "Plus, your boobs are a bit bigger, I noticed that yesterday but just thought you were getting your period." *Oh it speaks,* one of the voices in Everett's brain said to him.

Charlie nodded her head in agreement with his observation. "But how, isn't it nearly impossible for us, creating that, making that happen?" It is a rhetorical question from Charlie, she knew she was right. She remembers it quite clearly as one of the last updates she read online before the internet went a bit quiet. You'd get bits and pieces here and there, but for the most part there isn't any new updates or news or new postings. It still worked but, and in Charlie's case, she just didn't use it anymore.

Everett nodded to her observation. "Maybe you are just late and have a stomach flu to add to the coincidence. But we will go to the store ASAP. Actually, I will go to the store, you try to eat. You must be starving. Are you okay to make the food yourself while I am out? I will just go to the pharmacy and come back. Fingers crossed the tests aren't expired."

"Yes, I will be fine. Go, I will stay here in case I throw up again. And I need to eat, I am starving. I am sorry, I sort of blurted that out. Should I have not? You look upset. You are right, maybe I am just late and I am causing all this for nothing." As Charlie said

## Starting Again

the word *this*, she waved her hand in a circle in front of her to demonstrate the stress that she and Everett were feeling right now.

"I am fine, we will be fine. I will go get the pregnancy test and come right back. Don't move." Everett grabbed the truck keys and disappeared through the door. Returning not more than thirty minutes later, the truck screeching to a halt in the driveway, he ran to the house, bursting through the door, tests in hand. He practically threw them at Charlie the minute he stepped in the doorway.

"Here you go, I grabbed as many as I could find. Not surprising, but lots of those lying around the store. Grabbed some of these as well, also not in high demand so plentiful in supply." He was giving the pregnancy tests to Charlie and pulling boxes of condoms out of his pockets. Cargo pants serving since 1938.

There were two plates on the table, one had a grilled cheese sandwich and a fruit smoothie next to it, the other had crumbs. "Beware: I ate, so who knows when I will blow next." Everett sat down and pulled the full plate to himself and started scarfing down the sandwich. "Did you unhinge your jaw while you were away?" Charlie said, almost laughing. She is making jokes but also worried he might choke if he didn't chew his food.

Everett didn't say anything, but his eyes spoke a novel, and that novel is *leave me alone, woman, I'm starving and stressed out*. Charlie took the hint and said she is going to go pee on some sticks, leaving the room to walk to the bathroom, which is down the hall facing the master bedroom. The last room on the right. As she walked down the hallway, she kept telling herself that there was no way she is pregnant, she is jumping to conclusions. This is going to be fine.

Entering the bathroom she took four different tests out of the bag Everett had handed her and started reading packages. Thankfully, she did have to pee so this should be fairly easy. She would do this now and in the morning, just to be sure, as directed on some of the boxes.

As she is reading and unpacking, Everett appeared in the door, startling her. "Hey, whatever happens, I'm here for you. I may have froze there for a while but whatever happens we will handle it together. Like taking the tests, I'm here to help. So do you want me to hand them to you or take them from you? Pee doesn't freak me out, so your choice."

Charlie is warmed from heart to soul by his gesture and presence. So much that tears started pooling in the corner of her eyes. She wiped at them right away as there is no need for them, but nonetheless she is touched. "Okay, you hand them to me. You don't need to be exposed to all my bodily fluids." She leaned in to kiss him. "Thank you," she whispered while they stayed connected at the forehead.

Everett wrapped his arms around her and gave her a good squeeze. "Okay, let's do this!" And then he released her. Charlie, in an almost marching fashion, made her way to the toilet from the sink. She had lined up the tests along the countertop ready for use.

Charlie discreetly pulled her pants down to sit on the toilet; this is the first time she has peed in front of anyone who isn't her parents or sibling. She had had boyfriends, but to her recollection never at any point did the occasion arise to pee in front of them. It is strange but so is the situation. Charlie hesitated at first but relaxed to let a good stream form, stopping to place a test in the path and continue peeing. She did the stop and go four times, fairly mess-free if she did say so herself. And now they wait.

Each test had their own wait time, but Charlie had lined them up by longest wait time to shortest, so by the time they finished with the last test they wouldn't need to wait as long for the result to show on the first one. Everett is timing on his watch. They didn't speak. Charlie wiped and got up, pulling up her pants and standing next to him in silence. They looked at each other in the mirror not wanting to look down. Charlie biting her lip, and Everett tapping a finger on the countertop.

*Starting Again*

It didn't feel long enough, but Everett's watch beeped when the five minutes had passed. Still looking at each other in the mirror, they took a big deep breath in and when they had finished exhaling, nodded at each other and looked down at the same time.

Disbelief at first, shocked second, and then terrified. Those were the emotions in that sequence that passed through them both. Two plus signs, one pink line, and one that said "pregnant." All four tests indicated that Charlie is, in fact, pregnant. Charlie swayed a bit and then threw up in the toilet but this time probably from the shock and fear, less from being pregnant. Everett, sweet as always, held her hair and rubbed her back.

"Well, shit! First, I love you and second, what the fuck!" Everett spoke first after Charlie had finished throwing up and is standing again. "Okay, so you are pregnant, we made a baby. Holy FUCK." Everett seemed to be ranting a bit, but considering the news it is merited. Charlie is in shock, too, and just stood there nodding.

"Can we go lie down in the bed, hold each other for a bit, is that okay? You feel okay for that?" Everett sounded a bit frantic now but it balanced out Charlie's silence. She nodded and together, holding hands, they walked into the bedroom and got under the covers. At nighttime, Everett always thought the blanket was too heavy and made him too hot, but right now it is just heavy enough. He is in a cocoon with Charlie. It made him feel safe. They lay there, holding and spooning each other for hours.

# Chapter 20

## Together

A month has gone by, it is now July 11. Summer is in full swing, blooming, producing, and full of new life. Charlie is like summer, she is blooming and creating new life. But outside summer made inside Charlie sick in every way, every day since that fateful day a month ago.

Charlie did not just have morning sickness, she had lunchtime sickness, before dinner sickness, after dinner sickness, and while she tried to sleep sickness. Everett can't make Charlie anything that appeals to her or she can keep down. There are two options at this point, high-sugar popsicles or hot dogs. Two items that Charlie would not have consumed normally or at all, but for now that is it.

Charlie and Everett went to do a full supply run one day a couple of weeks ago and grabbed some books from a second-hand store. One of which is the famous one for pregnant woman. Lots of info on what to expect, tips and tricks, and when to worry about certain issues. They also grabbed an ultrasound machine from a clinic that is not in use. They also took the normal stuff like rubbing alcohol, bandages, and temporary stiches, to name a few.

They grabbed food, stuff for the farm and for the house. There were baby items but they both felt foolish taking that at this early stage of the pregnancy. They had worked out the math that Charlie is probably two months along. Everett had asked if she is sure the baby is his. Charlie rolled her eyes so hard it made her feel sick to her stomach and subsequently threw up. That put an end to that topic, the outing was hard enough, even though she insisted on going.

Everett has never complained once so far about taking on most of the work. He did burn the bodies from the cellar the day after he found out about the pregnancy, alone, and has since continued doing most of the chores himself. Charlie tries to do what she can but she feels so sick and exhausted all the time that she just ends up resting, reading, or a combination of both.

Everett pampers Charlie best he can and makes her hot dogs at two a.m. if she asks. Charlie is not used to being incapacitated, has made a habit of not being unable to do things since her recovery from cancer. Took on the motto to live each day and do things just because she can. So, this past month and a bit has been hard for her. That is not including the flux of hormones, making her cry for random reasons at random times. Last night at dinner she sobbed uncontrollably for a few minutes and it was done. No sad feelings, just tears.

Charlie is happy to find the pregnancy book, it gave her a bit of comfort about what she is going through. Although in the book what she is experiencing usually started a bit later in the pregnancy for most women, but the book also said that each pregnancy is different. Sometimes in the evenings Everett and Charlie look at the book together, learn about what size the baby will be at what month and when they can find out about the sex.

*Starting Again*

Everett has been doing as much research as possible on figuring out how to use and read the ultrasound machine, but mostly he has been keeping busy to keep his mind occupied. He often finds himself frozen mid-task to worry about not having a doctor, about the birth and about Charlie's well-being. The voices are louder these days with the added stress, and he can't help how stressed he feels. This is not a normal occurrence. Yes, in the history of the world women have been giving birth, but this is different. And they are alone.

The heat isn't helping Charlie, and she is due in February 2025, which seems horribly backwards to Charlie. You would want to give birth in the summer to have the baby comfy and be pregnant in the winter to have Mom comfy. Charlie often worries about Everett; he seems very preoccupied since he found out. They talk, but Charlie can sense that Everett is holding back how he feels to protect her from his burden. Which just makes it worse for Charlie because left to her own imagination, human nature dictates we go to the worst-case scenario. Charlie is worried Everett doesn't want this baby or her anymore.

But one thing had remained the same since the day they found out, every day before they ate dinner, around four p.m., they crawl into bed to snuggle under the blankets and spoon. Sometimes it is just for a few minutes, other times it is for many minutes. This eases Charlie's fears a little and Everett's voices go quiet for a while.

# Chapter 21

## Charlie

The sunset is getting later and later, as summer is in full swing. I sat on the porch at the little table Everett had set up for our evening tea or coffee. Coffee didn't make Everett hyper, it seemed to do the opposite and he is able to focus on a task much more easily. But I liked my tea, herbal chamomile. I had given up caffeine when I found out about the pregnancy.

This fine evening is no different, I sat in my wicker chair we found in one of the storage spaces, the garage or in the back of the barn. I have not been in the barn since my nightmare. I came to the door once and felt the same chill I had in my nightmare. Shivers ran from the top of my head down to my toes and so I decided to head back to the house. It is safe to say Everett got the table and chairs.

Sitting in the warmth, enjoying an evening breeze. It is about eight p.m. and I am alone, mesmerized by the beautiful colors appearing as the sun is going down. The peaches and oranges and the fuchsias. Fading up into a solid blue, cerulean blue, which later will turn into a dark navy blue and hold the stars for all to see.

My big belly takes up space but is not uncomfortable, I am simply seated further away from the table. I sip my tea and I am appreciative of the summer dress I found in the closet here at my home with Everett. Sweat pools under my ever-expanding breasts, between my legs and down my back, but I am happy. A calm washes over me. I am going to be a mother soon. I don't feel love for the little human in my stomach yet, but I am sure when he or she comes out I will fall madly in love.

The breezes are getting chillier, more brisk. And all of a sudden, unusual coolness for this time of year and time of evening. My exposed parts feel cool, my shoulders down to my fingers. My legs to my toes. I start to shiver.

I noticed the light is quickly fading, again as if black paint is being poured over the sky. I watch the light almost melt away to the earth. It is pitch-black. I scream for Everett who is nowhere to be seen. The porch faces the back of the property, which faces the fields and barns, and distant forest lined with mountains in the background. I cannot distinguish any shapes as I impatiently wait for my eyesight to adjust.

Screaming for Everett, I realize I cannot move, I am stuck seated in the chair. This makes me scream more for my beloved. I am scared now not only for myself but the baby I carry inside my body. I am the mother, my body will be a shield if necessary.

This is when the moaning starts, I can hear a faint moaning coming from down the field straight ahead of me. I cannot see anything. I think I see a person but it could also be a fence post. This moaning, I have heard it before. I am now on fire, the blood pumps at extreme speeds from my arteries to veins to my heart back throughout my body.

The moaning is getting closer and more piercing, it feels like it is piercing my mind and soul. As I strain to see what is making the

## Starting Again

moaning sound, I am struggling to free myself from the chair. It is as if I have been superglued down, arms to arms and body to body.

I can see movement, as if ten or more fence posts are coming from the forest and they are halfway across the field. They seem to be moving at a good pace.

There are multiple moaning sounds now, as if an opera singer got stuck on the first chord of the introduction song. Low and deep. It is not until they, to what feels like they, teleported to ten feet away from the porch from the fields, can I start to see it is people. Decomposing humans, dragging limbs along the ground, jaws unhinged and very little flesh clings to the bones.

I somehow know these creatures or who they used to be. They are moaning and excessive amounts of tar-like blood oozes from their gaping mouths. They are coming for me, for me baby, I can feel the imminent danger in my bones. "Stay back! Everett! Help me!" I scream.

I am screaming so hard I feel as though I have swallowed sandpaper, rough side on both sides of the paper. I am thrashing around to free my body from my prison, all the while they approach me, closing the gap to a foot away. They stop and just stare at me. I stop thrashing and stare at them. I recognize them, they are family. My mother and father, brother, grandmother, aunts, uncles, cousins. They are dead and I know they are dead; I watched the life leave their bodies as they gave up the fight against the virus overtaking their insides. I watched as they drew their last breath and the hand I was holding went limp. I sobbed and grieved their departure. Not only from this human plain of existence, but when the cleanup happened. I watched their bodies be taken away. Not knowing where they were going, nowhere I could go and visit them like a normal gravesite.

My family is here to hurt me somehow, and I don't know why. I started to sob again. I have missed them so deeply and am so scared of them at the same time. What they were going to do. Tears flowed down my cheeks. I can't stop the tears. I have so much pain and loss in my heart for those I loved, and I have shed a hundred tears for each person.

I stop fighting, I am exhausted from holding my grief inside and not letting it out. I am exhausted from feeling guilty that I lived and they died. Guilty that in their last hours of suffering I had wished they would just die to be free from the pain. Guilty that I could do nothing as three-quarters of the world just disappeared.

I start screaming in pain and sadness, and in agony. The corpses, the shells of those I had once loved and called my family, were tearing into my belly. Ripping the skin away, one layer at a time. Stabbing me with their long, dirty nails. Scooping out handfuls of my insides, digging for what they truly came for. I could hear a baby's cries, the sound is so vulnerable and weak. I am helpless to save my baby. I just cry and cry, looking away, not wanting to see what they were doing to my baby.

"Charlie, Charlie, wake up, you are dreaming again. Charlie, love, wake up."

Everett's voice is faraway, but then became a bit louder and louder. I could feel his hands on my shoulders and as if being sucked from one place and spat back into reality. I fully woke with a startle. Reaching out for Everett to brace my fall back into the real world, the awakened world. The zombie-less world.

# Chapter 22

## Everett

August 11. It has been three months of sickness and nightmares for Charlie. Nothing helps the sickness and Charlie has lost weight. Well, lots of weight and I am worried. I worry about a lot of things. The baby, me as a father, the birth, Charlie losing weight instead of gaining, getting stuff done, and trying to keep the voices away. If not for the pregnancy tests and the absence of her period, Charlie isn't looking pregnant, she looks like she has cancer again.

She has dark circles under her slightly sunken eyes, she hardly moves mostly out of weakness, but also trying to keep the vomit at bay. She rarely goes outside because the heat is too much for her so she is as see-through as skimmed milk. I worry, I worry a lot. I try to make her food, but that is a hit or miss depending on the hour. Neither of us sleep much at night; her nightmares are vicious inside and outside. She thrashes around with her arms and legs. It is like being on the losing end of a dodgeball game.

I try to hold her, to comfort her, to take on as much as I can so she can rest, and she is grateful but I'm not sure how much longer either of us can take this pregnancy. I have to be strong for us both right now and I feel like I am failing. All day and night I have negative feedback going on in my mind, running through every scenario and what I did wrong, how I could have done better.

The only peaceful time I get, we get, is our afternoon cocoon cuddles. That seems to be the only time we rest, we connect, and we feel safe. Charlie doesn't seem so sick under the protection of the sheet. It used to be a blanket until the weather became too warm for it. It is less weighted but still feels isolated enough to block out the voices, just for a little while.

That is my favorite time of day, laying close to Charlie, alone in the world. Just us, and in more than one sense of that statement. We are alone, not many humans live on Vancouver Island as it is, and with the pandemic we could spend ten years driving around and not meet another soul.

I love to feel Charlie's warmth, that is her sign of life to me. When she is the little spoon and I am the big spoon. I feel her heart and feel her warmth. I stroke her beautiful hair or rub her tummy, slowly. I don't want to upset her stomach. And for at least an hour we lay there, we don't have to speak to share our love for each other. We do it in touch.

Charlie is working so hard on creating life I don't want to burden her with my worries, so I try to do what I can to handle it on my own. Finding books and doing research on performing the ultrasound, which we will be doing today. Researching and reading on how to help Charlie give birth, what we need, what my role will be. What signs of trouble to keep my eye out for. That pregnancy book talks a lot about what to worry about during the pregnancy, an example they give is when the baby is placed feet

## Starting Again

first, a foot or two could come out first. I would say a dangling foot is definitely something to worry about.

On one of my trips out to get supplies in town, I was walking around looking for a baby store, or maternity store. I wanted to get some stuff and especially something nice for Charlie. She isn't showing now but when she does, I want her to feel pretty and comfortable. Walking around a deserted town is ominous and creepy. I don't like it; it feels end of days. The only bonus is that we don't have to pay for anything. And thankfully our crops are doing well because food is getting scarce here.

On my walkabout, I did find a maternity store and grabbed a few things at every size and for every season. I looked like *Pretty Woman* literally walking down the street back to the truck. But I walked by a jewelry store. I had never thought of proposing to Charlie, we sort of got thrown into this relationship. By fate it feels as though I love her with my whole soul, but I'm not sure how she feels about marriage. I hadn't thought about it.

When I was sick I thought about it a lot, but mostly as something that I would never get to do because I was dying. I felt sorry for myself that I would never be a father, or get married, have a life filled with happiness and memories. But now, ever since Charlie drove into my life, I find myself dreaming about these things again. And, well, one of them is already coming true.

So here I am standing in a jewelry shop filled with things people would have murdered their mothers for, free for me to pick the one I want, the one Charlie would want. I find myself smiling as I daydream about a traditional wedding: Charlie walking down the aisle towards me, looking as beautiful as ever. When I come back to reality I'm staring at a ring. As if it is telling me it is the one I've come here looking for. I walk behind the counter and take it from the display case. It is a beautiful white-gold diamond ring. A single stone but it shines like the North Star.

*Nathalie Edwards*

I know nothing of diamonds or proposing or being a husband, but I want it all with Charlie. And this may seem trivial at this point, there is no one to marry us, but I want this and I have no words to describe why. So, I take the ring and head back home. I don't know how or when, but I will marry Charlie Wolfe.

# Chapter 23

## Together

When Everett comes back from getting supplies, he gave Charlie the maternity clothes right away. He is more excited about the ring in his pocket but giving her the clothes for now will do. And Charlie is very grateful, she didn't need maternity clothes yet, but she thought Everett to be so very thoughtful in thinking of her and getting this on his supply run.

Charlie had been feeling a little bit better that day, she woke up feeling not like trash and even kept breakfast down. So by the time Everett had returned she already had it in her mind to give him a bit of a surprise. He has been working so hard and taking so much on to let her journey through this pregnancy up to this point, that she decided he deserved a little afternoon delight.

For as many times as they have had sex, she has not had much opportunity to perform oral sex on him, so hopefully this will come off as a gesture of appreciation and not as an obligation. She loved Everett so much and appreciated him even more. She could not imagine going through all this without him. She had known him only just over three months, but it is right and meant to be.

She never thought about kids. She was always too selfish or drunk, or a combination of the two. And when she was diagnosed with cancer and it progressed to terminal while in treatment, she buried any notion of ever having a normal life, marriage and kids, happy and thriving.

She didn't put much thought into it either since she found out she is pregnant; anything can happen and she didn't hold too much hope that this would go full term. And what scared her the most is doing this with no doctor. Our society is far beyond women giving birth in the fields, but if it has been done before, she will do what she can to do it again.

But back to Everett's surprise, she is feeling good and that is more than she had felt in months. It gave her a spring in her step and color in her face. She is excited to pleasure him, return a little to what it was like before, in that first month. The book she has been reading gives her hope that soon the morning sickness will end and apparently there will be a surge of horniness to be expected afterwards, but we will see. Maybe today is the start of a new phase in the pregnancy.

Charlie heard Everett pull into the driveway and excitement started to crawl from her stomach to her heart. Why should giving her, boyfriend—no that doesn't sound or feel right—partner, okay, partner, a blow job, make her so excited. She is excited to do something nice for him, that is her motivation and reward.

Everett walked in with such a big smile on his face as he handed her the plethora of clothes, and he starts to explain each of them. The why and the thought that went into each piece. Charlie is overwhelmed with love for his man standing in front of her, overjoyed by his expression of love.

"Come sit, sit next to me. These are all wonderful and wonderfully thoughtful. Thank you. I woke up this morning feeling much better, don't feel so thrashy, and I wanted to say how grateful I am that you have been taking on so much of the workload. Please don't think I take it for granted."

"I haven't been taking most of the load, I am just doing what I can to help you. You are nurturing the life inside you. Our kid. So don't think you aren't doing your share."

"Well, nonetheless I did want to thank you anyway, and I thought I could do that by giving you a little something." Charlie had moved closer to Everett on the couch where she had been sitting for the maternity clothes fashion show. She first leaned in and gave Everett a soft, loving kiss, just tenderness for his kind soul.

But once the kiss is over, she pushed him at the chest and guided him to lie down on the couch.

"What are you doing?"

"Just let me thank you. I want to give you something."

Charlie is undoing the button of Everett's pants. Everett fought for maybe half a second but he is pretty sure he could not change Charlie's mind, so he decided to enjoy the gesture. It is nice to see Charlie in a good mood, he is happy, she is happy. "Woah, ummm, okay. Oh my god."

Charlie dove right into her surprise. She took a half second to admire Everett and his penis. It is straight, circumcised, smooth, and handsome. Can you say a dick looks handsome? Because she really thought Everett's to be attractive. Everett is a grower not a shower, and boy he had lots to grow.

Charlie is watching Everett as she moved up and down, filling her mouth and then retreating. Going as far down his shaft as she could. She had just spent months throwing up, and as much as she wanted to please him, why tempt fate and accidentally gag herself. Ending the fun times.

Using her hand to cover the rest of the distance, Everett grew and became harder and harder. Physically showing his pleasure. Charlie added some twists at the tips when she is in retreat and swirled her tongue down along his shaft while she filled her mouth. Moving her hand up and down in sequence with her mouth, sometimes gyrating her hand in the opposite direction of her mouth for extra sensations.

Everett is groaning a low purr, and his hips were ever so slightly moving up and down with Charlie's motions, keeping in time. Everett's noises encouraged Charlie to keep going, adding a bit more pressure. Adding in the occasional very light graze of her teeth down and up his erection. And then sucking him back in with vigorous intensity. On occasion adding a deep thrust and a light pull out.

Everett is moving more and his verbal responses were louder now. Charlie could feel he is close to coming, and she wanted to watch him. Keeping a steady rhythm to help finish him off, she opened her eyes and looked up, Everett had his head back and had exposed his sharp jawlines and muscular neck. His head snapped back into an upright position and their eyes locked. Everett enjoyed that Charlie is watching him, and looking into her beautiful, deep brown eyes and seeing himself go in and out of her mouth threw him over the edge into ecstasy. Spewing his seed all in her mouth with a final push and grunt. Charlie could feel his body relax and his cock followed suit shortly after.

Charlie, again aware that she did not want to push her luck by swallowing his semen and upsetting her stomach, discreetly spit into a cup that had once provided her with a hot tea in the morning. She returned her attention to Everett who had not moved from his relaxed position, so she decided to join him. There is no sheet to cocoon them but they had each other and so she laid on top of him, her head on his chest to listen to his heartbeat. Strong and healthy, just like the rest of him.

# Chapter 24

## Together

"Before we start, do you want to know the sex of the baby?" Everett asks as he is setting up the ultrasound machine brought home a while ago and has been practicing with ever since. They haven't used it yet, and this will be their first time. Everett has been practicing on the animals, finding hearts and internal organs. But they wanted to wait as any other couple would until the three-month date.

Everett seemed bouncy, getting things ready, after his surprise. Charlie isn't sure what about blow jobs really made men happy, but she is happy that Everett is happy. "No, I don't want to know the sex of the baby. Do you?"

"I'm good not knowing, either. It will be a nice healthy surprise in six months."

"Agreed." Charlie is not surprised that they were once again happily on the same page.

"Alrighty, so you lay there and I'll get this thing started. It takes a few minutes. I've seen this used a few times in my career with the navy and I practiced on the animals. The internet is very helpful. So we should be okay. I can't guarantee I'll know where to go or if I can find the baby. The book said the baby is what size at this point?"

"Umm, three to four inches, I think, and we might not be able to distinguish the sex either. It can be hard as it is at this stage and we are no experts. Everett, I'm really worried about this. I haven't really had the time or space to enjoy the fact we are going to be parents because I worry constantly about not having a doctor or pediatrician. Neither of us have had experience or knowledge on how to deal if things aren't going as they should, in my stomach and out of my stomach. I'm sorry to put more on you but I had to tell you. I'm worried."

Everett felt relief and is reassured that Charlie felt the same. It gave him the space to share his worries, too, as similar as they are. "I have the same worries, and I am worried about you. These last three months have been hard on you. I just keep telling myself that we will figure it out as we go. I have lots of emergency response knowledge so that means first aid. The best that brings to the table is I know when we are in trouble because that would be when we hand off a patient to the higher authority, a doctor."

That did give Charlie a bit of comfort, she had forgotten his training and experience. "Okay, I guess I can't keep worrying about something that hasn't happened. I am ready, then. I'll be happy just hearing a heartbeat." Charlie laid down on an outside lounge chair Everett found with the other outside furniture, a smile on her face and lifting her shirt to expose her tiny belly. "Hey, we never really talked about if we are happy about this, or if it is something we wanted. You have been pretty withdrawn the last months. I was a bit too scared of the answer to ask until now, but the maternity clothes made it less scary, I think."

## Starting Again

Everett felt his heart hurt a little that she had noticed he is a bit internal with his thoughts and feelings, and that he hadn't said anything before. He felt a little ashamed to have listened so much to the voices in his head, telling him he isn't worthy, that he couldn't do this, that he didn't deserve happiness. Everett had been masking without knowing and now the mask is off and he started to cry.

Not sobbing, or overly dramatic, just tears of pain and relief started to roll down his cheeks. Almost cleansing. "I'm sorry, I have been distant. Just worried about everything and I'm tired. Not like you making a human tired, but I guess now realizing the same worries. I have thought about it." Everett wiped some tears away, even though more still came sliding down. "When I was dying I sort of killed those thoughts, never thought they would happen so why daydream about something you can never have. Then I was cured but half the world died. Seems like there wasn't much point in wanting something that seemed unattainable."

Everett moved from the ultrasound machine on one side of Charlie to a chair on her other side. They had this all set up in one of the spare bedrooms. Everett sat down, but something in his pocket poked him in the thigh. He had somehow forgotten about the ring in his pocket that he had picked up earlier today. He had no preconceived idea of when he would present this to Charlie, so he felt unprepared. But what he wanted to say next felt like a good fit for a proposal.

Everett didn't feel scared, he never felt more sure he wanted to do this than anything in his whole life. "Until I met you, everything felt unattainable. You make me feel loved and safe, you knock my socks off, and you are amazing woman. Until I met you, I didn't know what I wanted. So if you ask me if I want this baby, yes, would be my answer only because it is with you. If you ask me if I want to be a father, yes, because we will be parents together. Nothing in my life has felt more right than you and me, together."

*139*

Everett isn't sure why or if it looked silly, but he knelt down on one knee after taking the box from his pocket. "Charlie, I know things are not as they used to be, but my desire to be a family man is a real as it gets in these strange times. And I wondered if you would marry me, however that looks like now for us?"

Everett opened the box and presented it to Charlie, who is utterly blindsided by this proposal. Not unhappy having said that, just surprised. She was not expecting this, but she knew in her heart of hearts that she is one hundred percent invested in Everett and wanted the same things. Now she is the one with tears streaming down her cheeks and running into the creases of her folded neck from being in the horizontal position leaning on her elbows.

There is a moment of silence, but the smile on Charlie's face eased some of the fear growing in Everett. He felt good about asking, but also didn't think she would say no. Charlie could see that Everett is becoming nervous from his facial expressions, he carried them there even though he thought he is hiding them well.

"Everett, of course! However this looks for us, it is perfect and there is nothing I want more than to make this life with you and share it with you alone for the rest of my days. I love you, plain and simple, all of you."

Everett stood up to place the ring on Charlie's finger, it all seemed so old-fashioned but maybe that is just what they needed now, something traditional to balance out the uncertainty of all this newness. Both their hearts were filled with so much caring and affection and love for the other. Nothing could make the moment any more of a precious memory.

"I love the ring. I haven't really thought about what I would like in a ring, but this is perfect. And it fits perfectly, which is a bonus. Where did you get this?" Charlie is taking off the price tag as she spoke, making Everett feel embarrassed, but to be fair he hadn't planned to give it to her today, so he felt off the hook as they say for forgetting.

"At the local jewelry store in town today. I had some time to think about other things instead of worrying, and I just went in. As if being led by the goddess of love herself." Everett let out an awkward giggle that felt good, he was ecstatic that Charlie said yes and that she liked his choice in rings. That she hadn't thought him foolish for his actions or dreams for the future.

They embraced as comfortably as two could with one lying down and the other standing. Everett looking down at Charlie, in the lounge chair brought to the front of his attention the reason she is in that position in the first place.

"This is wonderful. I love you and shall we see if we can hear and see a baby in there?" he says, gesturing to her stomach. He returns to his original spot to see if he can make magic happen with the ultrasound machine.

"Yes, we shall!" Charlie responded as she is lubing up her stomach with the transmission gel that they found at the same time as the machine. It is cold, just like in the movies. Everett, ready with wand in hand, placed it in the space between her belly button and the top of her pubic area. "Here we go."

# Chapter 25

## Charlie

After hearing my baby's heartbeat, there is an instant connection. I loved that baby so much I would die to save its life, however that is to be. Today is the best day of my life so far, and I could not think of a better way to top it off, than by hearing and seeing the baby in my stomach. It took Everett a while to figure it out, but we had seen enough movies to know that the rapid blip blip blip on the screen is a heartbeat. After that we were useless. It could have had fifteen fingers and no toes and we would not have been the wiser. There is a baby and for now that is all we needed to see.

After the ultrasound, it is time for our afternoon cuddle. This day is just perfect. I hadn't thought about marriage or a family before but now that is all I could think about. And how lucky I am that it is all happening to me and Everett. He is so sweet and considerate, not to mention so hot and great in bed. That is not all the counts but it certainly helps. I might not know all his stories but I think I know him, and what I know of him I love.

While we cuddled, Everett had fallen asleep like he usually does. I could tell when his arm that is wrapped around my shoulder had slid off. The big spoon had fallen asleep and I didn't move a muscle. My nightmares keep him up so he needs a bit of recovery sleep. I am thinking about the book we got on what to expect during pregnancy. There is lots of information about issues that could arise with older moms, such as myself. All I could think about is how we would not be able to tell anything ever. There are so many routine tests done at different stages of the pregnancy that I won't get to take and give me some relief that at least that is one less thing to worry about. I get to worry about it all, for six more months. But for now the baby has a heartbeat so I'll take that as a win.

My second thoughts are if we are a bit of an anomaly in being pregnant right after the pandemic. I think tomorrow I'll continue that journal. I made one entry in back in May about how it is going, but it might be useful to someone someday.

As I am thinking about journaling, I am twirling my new ring around my finger. It truly is beautiful. I know nothing of diamonds and or wedding rings so my opinion is solely limited to saying it is pretty or not. Brillance, cut, and quality; your guess is as good as mine. I have never been so loved by a partner in my life, and I feel like Everett would go to every length of world for me if needed or I asked.

My stomach starts to growl a little and this time not because I am going to puke: I am starving. But there is another kind of hunger I am feeling, an old friend has come back. I am feeling horny, I have a strong desire to be penetrated, to be sucked and squeezed and scratched. Everett doesn't know, but about a month ago I found a vibrator still in its package in the closet. Maybe an

## Starting Again

unopened gift received or to be given, but I either way I don't care and I want to take it out for a spin right now.

I am a bit torn, because I want Everett to get some rest and on the other hand I might spontaneously burst into flames from this urge if I don't do something about it. Maybe I'll sneak off into the other room and masturbate and leave Everett out of this one. He had a little treat this afternoon, I think I'll give myself one, too. I guess I do understand blow jobs after all.

As stealthy as a ninja, or that is how I picture myself in my mind, I ever so slowly remove the sheet. Thankfully, the floor fan we have running provides a bit of sound shelter for when my feet hit the ground, the floors are wood and old. And they creak. My feet are on the floor but I'm still laying down, patiently moving one molecule at a time. I have never snuck off during our cocoon time so have no experience at this.

I remember taking a yoga class about ten years ago and the instructor had told the class that when we stand from touching our toes to really stretch each vertebra as we roll up. This feels like that; I am moving so slowly that my blood is stilled with anticipation.

Once I am seated, I slowly stand in the same fashion, and before I know it I am inching one toe at a time out of the room, grabbing my new toy before I leave. I sneak down the hallway and veer to the living room towards the couch. I am so hot and bothered right now I barely wait until I have my dress up and underwear down before getting this tiny ice cream cone–shaped device purring like a car engine. I figure out that there are speeds and different pulses pretty quickly, but enjoy the experimentation at the same time.

"Can I join the party?" Everett's voice scares me to death. I'm not embarrassed but I stop now just because my heart is racing from the shock.

"I am sorry, I didn't want to wake you up. I am just so horny all of a sudden. The day has just been the best in my life and while we were cuddling I thought I would burst into flames if I didn't have an orgasm. Sorry I'm blabbing, I'd love for you to join the party if you are feeling up to it."

"I will always feel up to it with you, and this scene is just so hot. Where did you get that vibrator? Never mind, I don't care, carry on. I'd like to watch you pleasure yourself some more."

I have never done this before but I trust Everett with my life and I can see the shape of his erection already in his jeans, so I can tell he likes this. I turn my vibrator back on and place it back on my clit. I do mini circles while I use the other hand to pull the skin away from my clit to expose it just a little more.

Everett stands up and takes his shirt off and his pants and sits back down on the chair facing the couch, where he had been watching me. He is fully naked in the light of day and what a specimen he is. He is muscular and lean, and I get to touch that and lick that all day and night.

Everett starts to touch himself, pleasuring himself while he watches me do the same. Seeing him so hard and seeing the delicious look in his eyes of rapture just turns me right on, even more so. I didn't think this would take long, but I'm thrown into hyperdrive, and my peak erupts suddenly and intensely. My release is satisfying, but I am ripe with anticipation when Everett gets up and walks towards me in all his glory.

I spread my legs to welcome him in, the last three months have felt like years. He kneels down on one leg and licks my opening and runs his tongue up to my swollen clit and gently massages it. Letting spit from his mouth run down his tongue and down the smooth space between my clit and opening. He stands up and with one foot on the ground and the other bent on the couch, he tugs me closer to him. Taking his cock in his hand he guides it right into me using his spit as lube.

Thrill radiates throughout my body like little shocks of electricity. I am still enjoying the feelings from my release and he is intensifying the joy by a trillion. I clench down on him, to feel him

*Starting Again*

more deeply. He is moving in and out, tantalizing each fiber of my g-spot with each stroke.

I wiggle a bit and turn myself over, leaving him inside me as I do, sort of like a roasting pig. I am on my hands and knees now and reach for my wand. Everett is obviously pleased I am using the toy at the same time, and I moan out of sheer ecstasy as he pulls my hair. He is thrusting a bit quicker and holding my hair, he leans back as if riding a horse, and he spanks me. This is new to me and at first I am surprised but it felt good and added to my pleasure.

"More," I said to him, and he spanks me again. It is not hard nor soft, it doesn't hurt and brings out more pleasure. He spanks me again, and again. I can hear him breathing hard and I am breathing harder. We are in sync and each movement is for the benefit of ourselves. Nothing is wasted in this moment.

He spanks me a final time and firecrackers burst into an explosion of satisfaction inside, causing my eyes to roll into the back of my head and me clenching down so hard I squeezed him out of me.

"I'm sorry," I breathe out.

"I'm not," he replies as he re-enters me and pumps in and out of me quickly. His hands are on my hips now and I can feel them squeezing me harder and harder until he gives that last thrust to the beginning of his orgasm.

# Chapter 26

# Together

The next morning, after a fabulous evening of being vomit-free, they play cribbage with breakfast outside. It is a lovely morning, warm with a breeze. Looking out from our porch at the land and all the animals and insects that inhabit this space is humbling. They were here first and appears they will be the last.

The sky is a pale blue without a cloud in sight. The blackberries that grow wherever they please, except where the goats keep them at bay, give off the most amazing floral scent from the ripe berries. The bees are busy collecting pollen and are almost golden in the sun's light, going from flower to flower.

There are flowers of all kinds around here, at this time of year they have blackberries, cucumbers, peppers, tomatoes, potatoes, and zucchini. Early season they had apples, cherries, peaches, plums, peppers, raspberries, blueberries, and beans. Their crops have done well, including many that don't flower either or you don't want to flower because that is the end of their productive phase like kale, swiss chard, lettuce, beets, and a variety of herbs. They have been lucky considering we started the seedlings later than indicated.

All kinds of bugs help to pollinate, and they'll have to rethink the crops next year as Charlie and Everett will most likely run out of flours and grains. Which is a bit more work to ensure they companion nicely together, whatever is grown close to each other.

Everett and Charlie are enjoying pancakes and coffee. Everett is counting his points from his kitty when he looked up to be stunned by Charlie's beauty. The early morning sun is striking her face at just the perfect angle; she is looking away, lost in her thoughts, golden highlights in her hair flowing over her shoulders, holding her cards to her seductive lips.

Every day she seemed to get more and more beautiful and thankfully she is looking healthier and stronger. Everett is happy to see Charlie eating and smiling. And he is very happy for her extra physical desires yesterday. A bit of normalcy after months of challenging changes

"Fifteen for two, fifteen for four, and a pair is six," Everett counted and pegged his points. Charlie's attention is called back to the game. She looked at Everett as if for the first time seeing him. He had kept the beard off and the hair short, all the more to see. She caught him looking at her in a way that the butterflies in her stomach fluttered before he looked away to count his points. Charlie is full of positivity today, she felt good and eating is so wonderful. She just had to remember to eat smaller portions but more often, the book had mentioned that it might help with morning sickness.

"It is so beautiful here, this, right now is living. The quietness and peace, yet noisy with life. The love and the company, life buzzing all around and growing inside. The smells in the air, the sun on our skin and the food in our bellies. This is paradise if you ask me. And I get to share it all with my betrothed."

"It really is perfect and so are you." Everett's feelings of love and admiration were painted across his face. He isn't very good at hiding his feelings, good or bad. Today it is good and made Charlie feel deserving.

"I know you are but what am I?" Charlie retorted, a twinkle in her eye. "How about we say you win this game, get our work done, and have a late picnic in one of the fields today. I feel fantastic and want to help with the animals and the plants. If I feel like it's too much I'll come back inside to rest. How does that sound?"

Everett is happy to see her spirits had been lifted, but didn't want to push their luck. "Ultimately it is your choice and leave it to you. Your body, your choice."

"Okay, well then, that is my plan, captain. Consider me your mate and off we go." Charlie stood up, more abruptly than she was aiming for, but her enthusiasm just sprang out like a bouncy ball sending her chair swiftly back. "It is going to be another good day, I can feel it."

Her gusto is contagious and infected Everett in the most excellent way. He had been alone for the last three months to work. It is way better with Charlie around. Not just for the extra hands to lighten the load but she silenced the voices in his head somehow. He cherished days like today, giggling and chatting with his love, stealing glances and kisses. Sparking their flames of passion just being near one another. It truly is a good morning and the time had skipped ahead without feeling it pass. It is noon already.

Charlie went inside to prepare some sandwiches, curried egg salad and added apples, nuts and some cheese slices to snack on. Charlie had wrapped and covered and put items in little baggies, and finally containing their delicious lunch in a portable cooler thing they found in a closet in the hallway. Content with her work of art, she gathered up the bag and went outside to gather Everett and walk to their unknown destination.

Charlie opened the back door that led to the porch, the hinges squeaking from age and probably rust. Standing at the bottom of the stairs is Everett, cleaned up and holding a bouquet of wildflowers. "My lady, shall we go picnic?" His hand stretched out, beckoning her to come down the stairs to him. Charlie placed her hand on her heart and could not stop the smile that grew on her face if she tried. It is a smile of awe. She is in awe and felt in awe about all this very wanted attention.

From there they walked hand in hand through the tall grassy fields to find the treasured spot under a big willow tree near the stream to the far left. Every bug lazily flew around in the heat of the day and the grass swayed gently with the breeze. Very picturesque. Everett set up the blanket, and once sitting down, Charlie spread the food to within easy reach. The flowers Everett gave her were in the middle on display.

They nibbled away at the sandwiches and snacks, joking and laughing at the silly things they each did. Everett appreciated Charlie's dark sense of humor and Charlie appreciated Everett's stories from his previous, post-pandemic life. The conversation is easy between them, and the silences were never awkward.

"Do you ever think things will go back to the way they were? I mean, being more structured, controlled by money, and working jobs we all hated," Charlie asked while gathering the rejected egg salad from the inside of the container with her finger.

"I don't know, probably. One day. We will need things we can't make ourselves. Or maybe not, who knows? If there aren't many of us making babies who knows what the future for the human race will look like? I could not want or need more than what I have right now," Everett continued. "Everyone seems peaceful for now, but human behavior has set a precedent to having been greedy, wanting more, and taking what they want at any cost." Charlie, having finished eating, had repositioned herself, laying on the blanket, listening to Everett.

## *Starting Again*

"There is so much unknown and it feels like so much is lost, but I don't think that is all necessarily bad. Maybe this is a good thing, learning and resetting the course of how we decide to live and exist with one another. But then we also potentially lose modern medicine, public transportation, security. It is overwhelming to think about sometimes," Charlie added from her place in the warm sun, basking in all its glory.

Everett is overwhelmed already with his worries of things closer to home. He didn't want to think of the future or continue with this topic. It is too much. Here on the farm, it is easy, you wake up and tend to the animals and the farm and you go to sleep. He could handle that right now.

In an effort to change the subject, to distract Charlie from her train of thought, he lay next to her. Scooping her in his arms and holding her. This will do for their afternoon siesta. Except Charlie's thin summer dress did very little to cover her body, and Everett had noticed she is not wearing anything underneath it. He could swear he could feel she is giving off a vibe or even a scent that she is interested in sex.

He couldn't see her face, but her body is doing some talking and he liked the topic of conversation very much. She had started to run her bare and golden tanned leg up and down his thigh. Her hand had started to explore the lines that surrounded his muscles, his chest and abs, as if she is learning braille or mapping out his body.

Charlie is not even conscious of what she is doing. She is lost in the dips of his muscular body, steady and protective. Even though he had washed up for the picnic, he hadn't showered, and his musk is alluring in a primal way. Her toes ran up and down his leg, unknowingly trying to ignite some flames.

Charlie found she could not go more than a few minutes this close to Everett and not be turned on. He is so intoxicating, stirring inner wants and needs just with his smell or proximity to her.

She isn't sure if this is the hormones from the pregnancy. but she desired him on every level at every moment. Desired to be near him, on him and him in her. All these that tugged at her inner sensualness were very persuasive and would not be denied when this man is hers, is close, and drew her to him like a magnet.

She had not noticed that her adventurous hands had made their way down to that V men have just at the bottom of their abs, leading down the treasure path. Everett is hard and his erection is what brought Charlie back down to earth. Her hand had brushed against it in her journey down his muscles.

She looked up at Everett who had fire in his eyes, and she gave into her urges. Not that there had been any reason not to, she just let them take over her body in this moment. Everett, who still had an arm around her, scooped her up in the arm and rolled Charlie on top of him, as if she was the rider and he the stud. Charlie started to rub her bare body up and down his covered erection.

She felt sensual, sexual, and free. She felt fearless and powerful. Rubbing herself up against the rough material of Everett's jeans is hitting all the right spots. She lifted her dress up and off her body over her head, exposing her naked body as she grinded her hips into Everett. The material billowed around all the curves of her body as it travelled over them. Being outside in the open is so erotic to Charlie, flaming her sex goddess confidence.

Everett, feeling restrained in his clothing and wanting to touch skin on skin all over his body with Charlie's body, raised his upper body and pulling from the back removed his shirt over his head. Messing up his hair along the way, Charlie liked how disheveled he looked. Crazy with passion for her. Everett brought Charlie to him while she continued to wind her hips against him. He kissed her nipples and tugged at them gently with his teeth. "Oh, Everett," Charlie whimpered with urgency.

Everett rolled Charlie and himself over in one swift movement so that he is now on top, gazing down at this spectacular creature writhing with lust for him. Removing his jeans and underwear as graceful as he could manage and returning his body to where it wanted to be, on top connecting skin to skin. He brushed her hair out of her face and studied her flushed face.

"I do truly love you and whatever comes our way I vow to never leave your side and work as hard on our relationship as I ever have on anything else in my life." Everett shifted his body to position himself so that he could enter Charlie, and did so slowly as he continued to talk. "I promise to do whatever it takes to make you happy." Moving in and out equally at about every third word, a Barry White pace of lovemaking. "I promise to take care of you and help you with whatever you need." The last word came out muffled as the pleasure from being inside Charlie caught in his throat.

Something in his words provoked something carnal inside Charlie, and she used her hips to roll herself back on top without Everett falling out. Everett placed a thumb over her clit, massaging it to heighten her pleasure. "And I promise to you to love you truly, madly, deeply every day. Making anywhere we are together a home." Now Charlie took up Everett's pace and she rose up and down on his erection. Maintaining eye contact, to watch the intensity build in his eyes.

"I love you with every fiber of my being and I would give my life for you. And I will do whatever I can to make you feel safe and loved for as long as I have breath in my lungs." The intensity of the blaze building in her body is becoming too distracting and stealing her breath from her words to continue.

Everett grabbed Charlie by the hips, to brace himself for the fury of his passion to explode with his impending ejaculation. He wanted to hold off a bit longer, but Charlie had taken a more assertive pace and he could no longer refuse his body the release to which he wanted so desperately. Everett had started becoming used to regular pleasurable moments with Charlie, the last three months felt deflated without her touch.

"Oh fuck," stuttered out of Charlie as she also allowed the desired ending to overcome her, coming with such severity, with what would only be considered the biggest orgasm of her life so far. Everett who is steadying her hips, growled as he also felt sweet release and came.

# Chapter 27

## Everett

I had started noticing that Charlie never wore shoes if the occasion didn't call for it. On our picnic, and sexual commitment coital event yesterday, which we should talk about at some point, she had not worn any shoes or footwear to walk the field. This is not the first time I had noticed that she is barefoot all the time inside the house, and really the only time she seemed to grace her feet with any sort of protection is to do chores.

It is mystifying and impressive what she could walk over with no really trouble. Rocks, prickly grass, and she didn't care too much about dirt or walking on pavement. I could never do that, the sensation of having something touching my feet or hands caused me to have anxiety. I wore gloves for any type of manual labor including washing dishes. Socks at the very least, but I really preferred having shoes or boots at all time outside. Inside I could live with socks.

Charlie is so different than me in most regards but similar in others. She could remember to close the cupboard doors, or turn off the light when leaving a room. She could start and finish a project without being distracted to start another. These are all things I cannot remember to do.

We both are similar in that we are stubborn, competitive, and know very random but sometimes useful facts about everything. I think Charlie compliments me in the areas where I lack and encourages me to be better in the areas that I am good in.

She is calm and even toned with emotions, whereas I am quick to react with emotions. I don't think either of us are perfect on our own, but together we fit like two pieces to a puzzle. Different but complementary. I had never experienced a relationship like this. Even with my family, we were never quite so in tune with each other.

I am done with the chores for the morning, I'm sitting on a fence beam, soaking up the sun. I've taken off my shirt to grab as much vitamin D from the sun as possible. I like to take moments, here and there to think about life and stuff, often it is planning for A, B, and C for different emergency situations. Probably from my military training, but I was like that even before. What I can't plan for is Charlie giving birth, and that scares me physically to death. Today thought I would much rather think about Charlie and how she doesn't wear shoes, and I love how different she is from me. I don't get it, but I love it.

I might also sneak in a thought about being a dad. I never thought in my wildest dreams that I would be a dad someday. I think about myself as early in my childhood as I can; I was always doing something I wasn't supposed to be doing. Breaking stuff by accident and breaking stuff on purpose. My parents tried to keep me busy with activities and sport to keep me out of trouble. I wonder if my kid will be as wild as me, boy or girl. I wonder if Charlie's antibodies against the virus that caused the pandemic will pass from her to the baby, also making the baby immune to the virus.

I have feelings of sadness pass through me like waves at the beach. That this kid won't grow up with friends to play with, or team sports to join. Who knows what things will look like in five to ten years from now, but as it is there are no schools or movie theaters. No parties or first dates, graduations, or a first interview.

This kid's life will be a whole other experience, and Charlie and I will just have to do all we can to fill in the gaps. Maybe we will have to travel or seek out others to give him or her or they the opportunity to see, touch, and smell life. I hope the baby gets Charlie's perfect nose and brown eyes and perfect lips. I read somewhere that babies look like the father so that in primitive times the father would be less likely to leave the mother and offspring. I don't plan on going anywhere and really hope the baby looks like the mother.

I gazed out into the lazy summer afternoon with mixed emotions, sitting on that fence beam for probably an hour. Staring at the mountain range that had just in the last days lost its snow peaks and patches. Everything is quite dry, with no rain in almost two months. Made me think that we should figure out a collection system for the fall and winter precipitation. Rain is the main season on Vancouver Island.

I was so lost in the schematics of the water collection system that I hadn't noticed Charlie approaching. Or heard her, no shoes makes for a silent walker. Scared me half to death when she hopped up onto the fence next to me. She leaned over and kissed my shoulder and then laid her head where she had kissed me.

"Hey, beautiful, you scared me. How ya doing?"

"I'm doing good, great actually. Few days now where I feel good if I eat little bits all the time. And you are looking like a mighty fine snack out here without a shirt on. Like a god sunning."

"I can't believe that out of anywhere in the world you could have traveled you came to me. What did I ever do to deserve such a fine woman?"

Charlie's reaction is certainly one of someone who is pleased with the compliment. I can read her expression pretty well now. Haven't seen anger yet but pretty sure that one will be evident. She is pretty honest and expressive. Charlie had a strange smirk on her face, not sure if that is lingering happiness or sass or what.

"What's that look on your face, you look like you are up to something," I asked but am unsure I wanted to hear the answer by the look on her face.

"Well, I have a surprise for you, if you would follow me, sir." Charlie reached out her hand to me, and both jumping off the fence I took her invitation, and she led me by my hand to the house.

She took me to her old house, the one that had the dead bodies in it. "Now go shower and put the clothes on that I set out for you. I promise there is a reason," Charlie said almost bubbling out of her skin with giddiness. I love to see how full of life and energy she is, the complete opposite of four short days ago. I comply with no objections; except I am less happy about going into this house but Charlie has made sure everything I need to shower and get dressed is here.

I run up the stairs, half out of curiosity as to what she is up to and the other half I expect some zombie to grab me from behind. Once there I do what I am instructed and shower, clean up, and put on the jeans and shirt on the bed. It's a bit warm for a long-sleeve shirt but it is made of cotton so shouldn't cook me too much. This is a bit fancier than I normally wear. I look at my reflection and shamelessly nod to myself in approval.

When I make it back down the stairs, Charlie is waiting for me at the door, in a white summer dress with her hair up, but she has little tendrils of loose curls framing her face. "You look handsome." I can tell she likes what she sees.

## Starting Again

"You look beautiful. Are we going on a date?"

"Something like that." And again she stretches out her hand for me to take, which I do, and she leads me to where we had our picnic yesterday. We walk in silence, the afternoon is so humbling in how peaceful life is here, the sun is out but not at full force. The animals and insects are present but not in your face. The tall grass is dry and makes a swoosh sound as it brushes up against my jeans with each step.

When we arrive at our destination, which I am not sure how I hadn't noticed on the approach, but the trees have sheer white material draped from branch to branch, flowing down in certain places. The material has intricate patterns of fresh wildflowers attached along the edges. There are bouquets of green ferns and long grass where the material is cinched to make that perfect R shape. Small tin buckets are filled with white painted sticks and ferns, lining the bottom of the trees and making a path from where we stop to under the willow tree. It is quite enchanting.

"What is going on?" This is all pretty elaborate for a date, but it is nice.

"Well, what we said to each other here almost a day ago made me want to marry you, and I know we can't do it like you may have wanted. I know things are different now, but I still want to marry you. Celebrate us. So, Everett, you feel like marrying me right now?"

"When did you do this?"

"When you were working. I was pretty sneaky and worked hard for you not to see me. Don't touch the sticks, the paint is probably still wet." Charlie chuckles and returns her gaze to me, still waiting for my reply.

"There is nothing more I want in life than to marry you right now, right here. Let's do it."

"I love you! Okay, so don't move, wait right here." Charlie disappeared under the tree for a few seconds and then I heard music start. It is Otis Redding, "These Arms of Mine," playing from the willow tree. Charlie reappears. "I remember you saying this is the most romantic song, seemed like a perfect song to walk down the aisle with. Shall we?" Charlie loops her arm through mine and gives me direction by motioning with her eyes that we should walk that way, that is the aisle.

"Shouldn't I already be down there waiting for you?" I lean in a whisper like we have a church full of people listening to us.

"Like this life I want to build with you, I thought we would walk down it together."

Emotions well in my heart and in the form of small tears in my eyes. I realized at that very moment that what I was missing in my life was Charlie. A person to do everything with. I nod in fear that if I try to speak I'll get all choked up. And so we walked down the aisle a couple of feet to under the willow tree. Grateful for that tree, it is warm in jeans and a shirt in the sun. The tree is the perfect umbrella.

Under the tree, to where the aisle ends, is a cell phone propped up amongst the lower branches playing the song. When we reach it, Charlie presses a button and it stops. Swiping, she hits play and a voice comes out: "Dearly beloved. We are gathered here today to witness the marriage of—" Charlie hits stop and fills in the blank with our names.

"This is great, I love you," I say to Charlie who just shrugs her shoulders but smiles and hits play again. The rest of the ceremony that you would have heard in the movies finishes out, we exchange vows, they are very similar to what we exchanged yesterday during our afternoon outside romp.

I can't take my eyes off of Charlie, her sun-kissed skin golden in the warm afternoon sunlight, her silhouette is illuminated by the sun shinning through the thin material of her dress. The tendrils of curls dancing with the light breeze. Her captivating brown eyes looking at me with such love, such devotion. The voice coming from the cell phone finally says, "I pronounce you husband and wife. You may kiss the bride," and so I do, I kiss Charlie with all my soul, my hopes and dreams. They are all hers, body and soul I am devoted to her.

"So it is official, your wagon is hitched to mine! Well, not so official and I'll be keeping my last name, but to me this is official enough to commit to you a hundred percent. Got it, buster?"

"Your wagon is the only wagon I would want to be hitched to, so got it," I reply. If we hadn't already made a baby, we would have made one that night. We consummated our vows, twice and once in the morning.

# Chapter 28

# Charlie

I wake up feeling saddened but comforted for some reason. I haven't had a nightmare in about a month now. It is now September 11 and I am four months pregnant. It is early morning, the sunlight is shining brightly through the window. The sun rises still way before six a.m. this time of the year. Everett is still sleeping so I am going to assume it is not six yet, that is when he usually wakes up. As I wake up, lying in bed, slowly remember why I am feeling sad and happy at the same time. I am staring out the open window, watching and listening to the birds and squirrels.

Bits and pieces of my dream last night are coming back, I dreamt of my family, those I lost. We were together here at the farm. I was much further along in my pregnancy and they were over visiting, congratulating me on my pregnancy and my wedding. My mom was sharing stories of her pregnancy and doting on Everett. She liked him a lot in my dream and I do think in real life she would have. She would have appreciated his kindness and affection for me.

My parents were kind and loving themselves. Not a mean bone in their bodies, and they loved the outdoors. Growing up we were always outdoors doing something fun. Rain or shine, the Wolfe family was hiking, biking, or camping. And my parents loved each other fiercely.

My dad, in my dream, was helping Everett set up the crib in the baby's room. My mom was telling me how proud she was that I quit drinking and finally met someone who I could build a life with. My brother was outside hanging with the animals, having grown up in the city, farm life was new and exciting for him. He was always a little shy and Everett was new so he was hiding to avoid making conversation. He grew to like Everett after some time.

And that was my dream, my family being here sharing this special occasion with us. Everett was happy, too, in the dream, just happy to be with people who cared about me and were overjoyed about the life we have created here. Happy for us and celebrating life, full of life.

I must have cried in my dream as I could feel the salty residue around my eyes. It felt amazing to be with them and they not trying to eat me or the baby. For them to be healthy and alive. An amazing and a sad reminder of what they will never be again. Sad that I can't share this with them, sad they will never know their grandchild. They will never spoil them and be there for the big moments, standing, walking, talking, school, first heartbreak, graduations, marriage.

Lying here thinking about everything I've lost makes me even more sad knowing that this baby will lose just as much being born now. What we have on the farm here will be lonely for a child or teenager, and I have no idea what life will look like at those stages. There are no schools or restaurants or kids to play with.

*Starting Again*

I am heartbroken for everyone at this very minute: dead, alive, or about to be born. Tears fill my eyes and start streaming down my cheeks, filling faster than my eyes can hold and overflowing. There is too much to lose in the world and it is overwhelming me with grief, and I feel betrayed for having been left behind to deal with all of this.

My tears turn into sobbing and I can't hide them under the sheet. Everett wakes up, alarmed at the sight of me, in my state. "Oh, babe. What's wrong, are you okay?" he says to me, scooping me up into his arms and pulling me into a tight hold.

I nod my head because I can't speak any words, opening my mouth would just let blubbering out. I am physically fine but mentally I feel assaulted. He squeezes me tighter, holds me until I just don't have any tears left and my body stops heaving. I feel like I have shed a tear for every lost soul and just a few extra for all that my baby has lost without even knowing it yet.

# Chapter 29
## Together

It is October 11 today, and Charlie is five months pregnant with a tiny little bump to show for it. Despite being a big ball of emotions, usually melancholy emotions, she is feeling healthy physically. She can't shake the feeling of immense loss even though she is creating life and had started to build a life with Everett.

Everett, as always, worried about Charlie, this is his first experience with pregnancy as well, his first baby. He and Charlie read the pregnancy book together, both having an appetite to know what is going on at this stage. Apparently, they will be able to feel the baby move soon and that will be exciting. They check weekly for the baby's heart rate on the ultrasound machine. Everett is getting pretty good at working that thing.

Everett sometimes felt that he became paralyzed when he had too many things to do in a day. It became crowded in his mind and it is a struggle to pick one to start with. Charlie played a key role in creating a safe environment where Everett could share what is going on. Charlie had walked in on Everett tapping his head one morning while doing chores. He clearly was working through something.

Everett was upset that he couldn't remember to do certain things, or get going, or he got lost in a certain task for long periods of time. Charlie held Everett and told him that she would help him, that they were a team. Ever since then he talked to Charlie about everything and he felt, for once, that it would be okay. That he is okay. She is his rock and he loved her deep into his being. That feeling seeped into every day they shared together.

Everett stands in the early morning by the greenhouse, watching Charlie harvest whatever had been ready. It is cool this morning, the summer is leaving the mornings and letting fall's cool intentions take place. Soon it would be time to get ready for winter. Everett is leaning in the doorway of the greenhouse structure, an arm up above his head to support himself, admiring Charlie. Soaking her in in all her beauty. Her shapely body bent over harvesting zucchinis. Her hair flowing across her shoulders. Her hair had become even more thick and luscious since becoming pregnant. Everett doesn't know where his obsession started with her hair, but he just got all worked up whenever it fell in her face or she let it down from being tied up. He wanted to tie her up.

Charlie happened to look behind her while Everett is having that very naughty image run through his head and gave him a quick smile. "What are you doing peeping on me like that? There is enough work for two here you know."

"I am picturing you with your arms above your head, tied together to the headboard. Your legs spread and your feet tied to the bottom posts. You are naked except for a blindfold covering your eyes. Your hair is braided and laying across your breast. I am running your wand vibrator along your body, from toe to ear, teasing you with it. Vibrating it along your nipple. I want to punish you for being bad. You need to be taught a lesson."

## *Starting Again*

Just talking about what he wanted to do to her, forgetting all his worries, he started to get hard. His growth is visible enough for Charlie to notice it through his jeans. She became instantly aroused at his arousal. Forgetting about the weight of her sadness.

She rose and turned to face him. She did not approach him, just connected her eyes with his. "And what next, what would you do to me next?"

"Next I would place your wand on your clit, working you up into a frenzy. Stop when you would get close. I'd run my teeth along your breasts and inflict pleasure to your nipples with the edge of my teeth. When you could take no more, I would untie your hands and feet, and flip you over so your bottom is presented to me like a gift. Touch the smoothness of your skin, but I would see the hue of your skin is too pink and not red enough. So I would spank you, hard, to give it some color."

Charlie, stood in her spot practically drooling. Stunned by her insatiable need to have Everett do exactly what he is saying to her. Everett was a bit surprised at the theme his mind had taken. Not surprised he is thinking it but surprised he is saying it. But it is how he is feeling and if he is going to share this experience with anyone it would be his wife.

Charlie started to braid her hair, as a signal that she is a hundred percent on board with today's extracurricular activities. Not how she saw her morning going but is thrilled at how it is turning out. Everett slowly made his approach towards her, stepping over rows of produce while she braided her hair. It is like a siren's call to Everett, his impulses were taking over. His blood now boiled with wants, wants that could only be satisfied by bringing Charlie to the edge and making her beg for sweet release.

These wants made Everett feel in control, calmed his mind like when he was part of the navy. The adrenaline gave him laser focus and a clear mind. Everett stepped into the role of dominant, his eyes grew dark and fire red at the same time. Charlie practically

*171*

melted at how hot he looked right now, how those eyes stirred something in her. Her stomach is all in knots at the excitement and the uncertainty, the unknown. She had never really engaged in this type of sexual activity. She never really trusted someone enough to share this intimate act with. She trusted Everett and gave herself to him fully without even a second thought.

Everett could sense that Charlie is offering herself to him in this capacity, and his gaze warmed a bit with how tenderly he felt towards her commitment to him. But that is a quick flash, his soul-piercing gaze grew even darker.

"Come here," he demanded in a stern and confident voice. Charlie did what he asked of her, she closed the gap of a foot that had remained between them. "Good girl." Everett slowly wrapped her braid around his hand until no loose hair could be found and in squeezing his handful, it tightened, forcing Charlie's head to tilt back to relieve the some of the pressure of the pull. Everett licked Charlie's chin and released the pressure he had on her hair, allowing her head to come to a normal position.

"No talking, the only word you are allowed to say is *stop* if you want me to stop. Do you agree?" Charlie nodded in agreement, demonstrating she understood the rules of the game, and unconscientiously bit her lower lip in a moment of uncertainty. An action that drove Everett crazy on the best of days, today is no different. It always made him want to bite her delicious lips for her.

Releasing her braid, he gave her instructions to go to their bedroom and watched her walk away. Something else he noticed is Charlie never wore a bra or underwear anymore. Her work clothes moved in certain ways to give a sneak peek into her top, and as she walked away he did not see any lines in her leggings. This woman is wild and she is all his. He would never let anyone touch her, ever. A growl grew in Everett's chest at the thought of others wanting what is his. Fuel for his fire. He made his way shortly behind Charlie into the house.

## Starting Again

Once inside, Everett found Charlie in the bedroom as she was told. "Take your clothes off," he said, giving her a smoldering glance as he started to undo his belt as she undressed. Everett slips the belt out of the loops in his jeans and calls Charlie over. "Put your hands together and put them out." Charlie does as she is told. Everett wraps the belt around her wrists and cinches it, trapping her hand like handcuffs.

Charlie takes a quick breath in and the rest plays out as described to her in the greenhouse. And so much more. Her butt cheeks were not the only ones left with a bright shade of coral. Everett never slapped her there, they were flushed from strenuous work and intense pleasure. Both their aches were eased.

# Chapter 30
## Charlie

Fall is in full force, as apparent on this rainy day on this eleventh day of November. I am six months pregnant, and lots has happened over the last month. After that memorable morning exactly a month ago we felt the baby move for first time. It isn't much but it is enough to keep our moods high and rosy for the rest of the day.

When I had asked Everett what had brought on that change in his sexy playtime, he told me that he felt in control in a way he hadn't felt in a while. We both feel so little control on most parts of our lives. Made me wonder how much actual control we had before the pandemic or was it all false. They say ignorance is bliss but I think knowledge gives us a false sense of control to a certain degree. Having access to a doctor does increase the chances that I will have a healthy pregnancy and safe birth, but how much control do we really have? Babies are born breach, early or late either way.

Everett, having come from such a structured background, is struggling to this new way of life. The farm life was good, it was quiet and rewarding busy work, but the only stimulation and structure is what he brings to the work. Having me here with him has helped, he feels safe and valued, he can be himself as a couple but there are too many variables he has no control over. The pregnancy is hard and he worries about the life this baby will have. The future is so uncertain. So being the dominant one gave him excitement and a sense of control.

We had done a big supply run, spanning over three days about two weeks ago. We got all we could to put together Everett's water collection system, first aid supplies, gardening supplies, and we finally got baby stuff. We got a crib, itty-bitty clothes and diapers, bottles and blankets, mobiles and play chairs. I'm finally starting to show a little bit, I have a tiny bump. Cocoon time has now turned into belly time; we rub the belly, talk to the belly, and wait for a response from the inside.

During our outing, I ran into a bookstore to get baby books, parenting books, and homesteading, and I grabbed some books on mental health. It is becoming apparent to me that we were both needing a bit of help dealing with all that happened. And this is not within my wheelhouse so I grabbed a few books. Everett laughed at me that I had carried my weight in books to the truck. It is how I have been spending my free time.

I am mostly interested in the mental health books, but I enjoy reading in general. I never did much reading when I drank, hard to read when you can't see straight. I know Everett is struggling with the loss of control, and I am, too. This is a new world but I'm more worried about the unpredictability of it all. Which feels very similar. And on the same coin I couldn't be happier with this gift of the luxury of time. And I am sober and using that time with purpose now.

## Starting Again

Reading these books have helped me recognize the whys and whats and hows, it helps me deal with all three in a constructive way. Either that or my hormones are evening out, which, who knows. I think of Everett every once in a while when I hit certain topics.

I am sitting in the living room, we have a fire going, and I am reading. Everett comes to join me after taking a shower. He has found some relief in going for a run after eating dinner and I have taken up yoga before I go to sleep. We are taking a healthy approach to our dealing with our feelings.

"What ya reading, lovely?" Everett asks as he walks into the room, taking a detour to the fireplace to put more wood in to fuel the heat.

"I am reading a book on mental health issues. I find it interesting, and there is a section here on alcoholism and drug addiction. You know, a little light reading before bed."

"Huh. I thought you were reading a murder mystery last time I saw you reading. This book telling you anything about yourself that you didn't know before?" Everett asked me, as he sat down next to me. He is never far from me when we were in the same room and never for long if we needed to do something separate.

I have been reading a lot about ADHD, PTSD, and anxiety, this is my thought on how Everett's brain has been wired. He has many of the indicators. I have no idea if he has ever talked about it, put himself in that category or would even care to know, so I keep my diagnosis to myself. I just read about how I can support him and guide him when needed.

"I was, I'm done that book. When I was drunk I never had much time for reading despite really enjoying it and wanting to do more of it. Not enough to stay sober, might I add. So I find this luxurious to be able to read as much as I can whenever I want. I have a few books on the go." I adjust my position on the couch. I want to face Everett, so I shift my expanding body and place my

*177*

book on my lap, facedown and open to keep my place. "As for me and learning about me, I knew I was an alcoholic well before I quit or got sick. So not really learning much. But it is a good reminder why I now choose not to drink anymore."

I rub my little hump unconsciously, grateful to have quit and survived so that I could be here, right now carrying my child and with a man I love. Everett jumps into the belly rubbing, he never misses the opportunity to rub the belly. Seems to be his new favorite pastime.

"Do you miss drinking?" he asks me, concern hiding behind his eyes. I'm sure he's had enough encounters with booze hounds to fill a lifetime with his job in the navy, saving our sorry asses at sea.

"I do not. I have had time to work through those feelings since this all happened. My life is much better without it and I refuse to let anything jeopardize what I have now."

Everett kindly put my hair behind my ear, a strand had fallen when I looked down at my belly as I spoke. "What were you like, if it isn't too hard to talk about?" he asks me, compassion replacing concern in his eyes.

"Well, I wasn't a very nice person, I had no control and made poor decisions is the generic answer. When I was younger I used alcohol as a social lubricant, which often led to bar fights and sleeping with random people. As I got older drinking just seemed to be my life and I was that person who was drunk at my godson's birthday parties, the only one drunk." I paused for a second.

"There was this time we were on a boat and my godson was ten. He was afraid to jump off the side with the other older kids. This was a fantastic example of the don'ts when it comes to day drinking. I grabbed him by the arm and chucked him over. He had a life jacket, but he was still scared and grabbed my hand as I was letting go of his. He ended up smashing into the side of the boat and hurting his arm. Didn't break anything, thankfully, but I certainly didn't help with his fear of jumping off the boat. I wish he was still alive for me to apologize to him for all the stupid things I did that caused him any harm."

Shame filled me from the inside out, and I am a bit embarrassed for having told someone who was not there that story. Or didn't know me then. "Don't be embarrassed, we all have our baggage and things we wish we could take back," Everett said as he snuggled closer to me and put an arm around me. How he knew I am embarrassed is a bit scary, but at this moment I am just happy he isn't judging me.

"And when you say *lots of people*, who and how many are we talking about?"

I couldn't see his face when he asked me but I could tell by his body language he is a bit nervous to ask that question. "I don't know a number but more than the average bear, I guess. Men and women, wasn't too picky. I have been tested for every STD on the planet, many times, so don't worry." More shame in having to add that last statement. "How about we talk about something else, how was your run? Must be getting darker each time you go out?" I ask, hoping he takes my bait, my attempt to change the subject.

"It was good, I feel a bit stronger. And it is definitely getting darker. Won't be able to keep doing this for much longer. Maybe we can find an indoor exercise machine next time we go out."

"Oh, I think I saw an exercise bike in the other property's garage. We should take a look tomorrow," I share with Everett, hopefully it works and gets the job done. I touch Everett on the arm to make sure I have his attention and ask him if he put his running clothes in the laundry room like I asked him when he started running. Makes my life easier to clean those first as their variety of stink leaked into the other clothing.

"I did, thanks for checking in with me."

# Chapter 31

## Everett

I didn't sleep much that night. I got to thinking about my past. I really appreciated Charlie sharing a little bit of her less than admirable moments. It just got me to thinking. I had one past serious relationship that almost led to marriage. But when I went into a jewelry store back then it wasn't like when I did for Charlie's ring. I stood there, still and glued in one spot. We had been together for a year and it felt like we both thought it was the right next step, but there was something that kept flashing in my mind that it never felt like the right next step to me. I never did buy a ring, and I got sick and she left.

She who shall remain unnamed and will be referred to as "she," is so different from Charlie. Or I guess should say *was*, I don't think she was a survivor. I feel as though all this shit had to happen so I could meet Charlie and start this life with her. Charlie is kind, patient, and I can be myself around her. "She" didn't take the time to understand how I work or try to find a way for us to both be happy.

Charlie doesn't get angry when she has to remind me to do things. Charlie doesn't throw it into my face when she finishes a task I got distracted from finishing. Charlie loves me more than just for my good looks or stellar performance in bed ("she" statements, not mine). Charlie has never called me stupid or lazy.

Now, a thought has entered my stream of memories. I did know "she" much longer than Charlie, but even at the beginning of that relationship with "she" it wasn't great. I felt instantly connected with Charlie. As I reminisce and compare, all of my most regrettable moments where I was most embarrassed bombard the rest of my waking time.

That awkward thing you said to your boss to seem normal, the overshare of your life's story at a party that was filled with people you didn't know. Accidentally walking in on your friend's spouse in the tub bathing their little kids. The walking in part wasn't the embarrassing thing, that was truly a mistake, but taking a good look at their goods without realizing you did and saying nothing, not even a simple "sorry."

Or that time that you went in for a kiss too quickly and bumped teeth. Nothing ruins a moment more than that person unsure of themselves and acting all nerdy about it. Spitting when you get to the exciting part of your story. All the missed opportunities, awkward encounters usually involving some bodily fluid, or all the stupid things you've said because you are having an internal monologue during a conversation.

I turn over and watch Charlie sleep. For all the stupid shit I did, I did right so far by her. I rub her belly and swear here and now that I would give my life to save both the humans sleeping next to me. I would murder the remaining million people on earth to get to them, to save them, or to seek revenge for hurting them. If anyone lays a hand on either of them I will make John Wick look

## Starting Again

like a preschooler. That is my solemn promise at this time on this day, on all that makes me whole, that I will be the worst villain in your story if anyone hurts my babies.

    I get up at this point to start the chores, no point lying here getting angrier and angrier at the fictious scenarios I can't stop myself from making up in my mind. I leave Charlie sleeping soundly and warm in our bed. Any anxious anger fuels the effort I put into my work even before the sun comes up.

# Chapter 32

## Together

Charlie hits the sixth month in style. Charlie is also not blind to the historical date markers her pregnancy are hitting either. September 11: when the airplanes hit the World Trade Center. It was a tragic day, and so many lives were lost in the most horrible way. November 11: Remembrance Day when we remember all that our relatives fought for. Our freedom and luxuries. Today, December 11, has none, but still a day to remember.

Eleven is Charlie's lucky number despite those dates and what they represent. Charlie always looks at the clock at 11:11 a.m., not that anything good or bad happens, she just looks at the clock at that time almost every day and has since she was a teenager. So it's not really a lucky number but just more her number.

September still had some nice weather, but December is really starting to feel like winter has arrived. It is dark early now, rain is the main weather forecast for the next four to five months, and it is cold. Cold here is not like cold everywhere in the world. Cold here is 3 degrees and that is usually only at nighttime.

The big blanket has come back out on the bed since October; much better for their daily afternoon cuddle conferences. Charlie has moved into the warm maternity clothes Everett found for her, and she also just wears his sweaters when appropriate as they still fit and are comfortable. They are into making soups and stews to feed their souls, and thankfully, Charlie has been able to eat pretty much anything since month three as long as there are snacks in between.

Charlie's bump exploded and is now half a basketball size. With the bigger tummy comes the breast fairy. Everett likes her, the breast fairy. And also a variety of interesting pregnancy phenomena such as dark skin patches in her armpits and along her belly. There is gas and upset stomachs, too, but all of the above is worth it because now the baby is really kicking and moving. A great source of entertainment for Charlie and Everett to watch and feel.

The baby growing inside her is now approximately twelve inches long and weighs about 1.5 to 2 lbs. That blows Charlie away at how small the baby is and hopeful for a small baby to push out of her when the time comes. And despite this baby being that small, Charlie's belly is not in proportion solely to the human in there. She can no longer see from the belly button down when standing straight. She has only gained belly weight, but she seems to be able to stay active enough to keep the rest of her the same size. Not that gaining weight during pregnancy is bad, just how it is going for Charlie.

Charlie has had to ask Everett for help with personal maintenance issues, lady scaping issues. She can no longer comfortably see her pubic area to take a razor to it. A lady has standards and Everett and Charlie still have pretty regular sex these days. It is not as S&M as it was a while ago. Everett is scared of hurting the baby, but nonetheless, Charlie feels like it is important to keep things

## Starting Again

tidy for everyone's enjoyment. So every week Charlie lies down on the bed they use for the ultrasound machine and he gives her a shave like an old-time barber. Everett could care less if Charlie is clean-cut or sporting a mullet down there, but he likes how she trusts him enough to hold a razor that close to her sensitive parts.

Outside of the growing belly, everything runs the same. There is no garden but Everett worked hard last month to get his water collection system up and ready for the rainy season. The animals are mainly in the barns now and will have enough feed for the winter, but that will most likely be the end of that. This winter will most likely be the end of many things, like available frozen food. That is why Charlie spends most of the day preserving what she can. And even learnt how to preserve eggs to last a year.

They do plan on using the cold storage under the other house. It seems to have worked well so they have stored carrots, onions, beets, and potatoes down there. They add their jarred food as well. Both of them get freaked out going in there and never go alone. It is a group effort every time.

Charlie stopped having nightmares back at the third month mark, too, thankfully, and that gave her the courage to go in there. If she was still having those nightmares there would be no chance in hell she would even set a foot inside the front door.

Everett is enjoying the stationary bike they found; keeps him calm and focused. He is so tired at the end of the day that he has no choice but to shut down instead of thinking about the past, thinking about what he needs to do tomorrow, or all the things that could go wrong with Charlie, the pregnancy, and the birth. It is good, because Everett feels more in control of his thoughts and how negative those thoughts used to get.

Today is no different than any other, the couple woke up at six a.m., had breakfast together, and Everett went outside to feed the animals while Charlie returned to preserving what she could. She has learnt how to make a decent loaf of bread. Flour is something else that is dwindling quickly in supply. But for now they will be fine. They have talked and will most likely have to start taking further trips to seek supplies. Days instead of hours. Charlie is scared to leave her home but it needs to be done.

It is three p.m. now, Charlie and Everett are in their cocoon talking baby names.

"For a boy, James, and a girl, Jasmin," Everett counters Charlie's suggestions of Peter for a boy and Evelyne for a girl.

"I like those, but how about Max for a boy or Nicole for a girl?"

Everett thinks on it but he still prefers James or Jasmin. "Not bad, but still like my J names better."

"You are sticking with those, huh? Well, I don't hate them but I think we should keep thinking on it and revisit the topic at a later date." Charlie adds a smile to soften not loving Everett's top pick in names. It is dark under the blanket but there is a splash of light coming from the top of the blanket at their heads. Everett sees Charlie's smile, knowing full well that she doesn't love the names but doesn't want to hurt his feelings. That is love right there.

"I guess we will just have to see when the baby comes and see what she or he looks like, a James or Mike or Beatrice."

"Beatrice? There is no way we are naming our baby Beatrice. My great-grandmother's name is Beatrice." Charlie is almost offended at the name but quickly realizes that Everett is just bugging her and enjoying riling her all up. They laugh and poke at each other for a while longer, until both their tummies let them know it is time to start making dinner. Lunchtime treats have long been digested.

# Chapter 33

## Together

Charlie finds herself alone and scared. Everett has left for a couple of days to widen their perimeter to search for food and supplies. A week ago Everett approached Charlie on the topic, they had a lengthy discussion on the pros and cons of the timing, and whether Charlie should go. It is still an unknown world outside the fences that outline their homestead.

Everett's main point for cons is that because he didn't know what to expect himself, he didn't want to put Charlie in any unnecessary harm. This is potentially his only chance to have his DNA out there, and Charlie is doing all the heavy lifting right now carrying this baby. He couldn't live with himself if something happened.

Charlie countered with the lack of evidence that something bad wouldn't happen here while he is gone. Charlie refused to be separated. Everett agreed he could not stop anything bad from happening here but why increase the odds of both of them dying if they were together. It isn't like Everett to be separated from Charlie but in this instance it felt right. He couldn't explain why.

The remaining points that Everett made were: the animals needed to be cared for, the snow would come soon so it is now or in the spring, he didn't want to leave when Charlie is closer to her due date, and the longer they waited the more food would spoil. Charlie did not protest those points; she is very unhappy with the major one of being separated.

Eventually, Everett convinced her on the point that the animals needed to be fed and could not be left and promised he would not be any longer than two days, one night. He could get to the bigger cities closest to them on the island in that time. He would bring the truck and trailer, and she would keep her car if she needed to leave.

They figured out a meeting place if she needed to leave and she if is not at the house when he got home. If the car is not in the driveway he would know she had left and would go straight there. In times like these they both wished that their cell phones still had any data, but that seems to have expired a couple of months ago. Apparently renewing your contract did not happen automatically.

He had left this morning and Charlie found as nighttime approached, she became anxious and frightful. She wished they had dogs to keep her company but they had not seen any free roaming domestic animals on any of their trips out. Charlie is trying to calm herself down by doing her yoga after dinner. She had spent the day doing chores and baking and cooking to keep her mind occupied. Reading is not strong enough to keep her mind's focus on the words, so she skipped reading and went straight to yoga, which is also doing a poor job but there is structure in her routine that helped. She had no idea how she would get any sleep tonight.

Today is December 11 and days are getting shorter and the darkness is getting longer. Which had never bothered her before

*Starting Again*

but tonight is different. In Charlie's mind evil lives in the darkness only, and if she could make it to morning she would be fine. All the doors and windows were locked, curtains closed, and she decided to add additional barriers by the doors with a stick in the tracks of the sliding door and old shower curtain, the adjustable pole type, that she placed and adjusted tightly between the small walls of the entryway.

With yoga and security detail out of the way, Charlie figured she should attempt to go to bed. It is earlier than she is used to, but still a reasonable time of nine p.m. She would need to get up early to feed the animals again. The cell phones didn't work for calls or text messages, but still is useful for taking pictures and listening to music. Showered and in her pj's, Charlie hesitantly pulled the blanket back and crawled in.

Her belly had continued to swell to accommodate her growing baby, so simple tasks were becoming a bit more physically demanding, such as getting in and out of bed. She could not imagine how big she will be by the time she reaches the nine-month mark. At this rate she will be a hot air balloon.

She navigates getting into bed, after turning the bedroom light off but left the door open to let the hallway night-light shine in. Music is on, a lovely selection of slow classical music on low to make a white noise background. Charlie can't stop thinking about Everett and hopes he is okay. It has been since she was a child that people didn't have a way to instantly stay connected. Being detached from the world via the internet is vastly different than not being able to check in with the one she loves.

It takes a while and with some effort to shut out the thoughts from running wild in her mind and she feels like she is finally able to drift off to sleep. She is warm and safe in her blanket but uncomfortable laying on her back, under the weight of her stomach. She turns over and the baby starts kicking her relentlessly. "Calm down, little person in there, it's time for sleep," she says and shushes in the effort to comfort the baby.

Preoccupied with soothing the soccer player she is carrying, Charlie thought to herself *I guess I'm not alone, I have you*. Finally settling into a space of security, physically and mentally, Charlie closes her eyes.

Charlie feels the blanket at her feet move when she didn't move herself. She jerks her head up and looks down at her feet. There is nothing, but it felt like a cat had jumped onto the bed. Her heart has sped up a bit with the adrenaline injected into her blood. She is grateful the light is on in the hallway outside her door but she feels inexplicably vulnerable with it open. She is torn between having a light on or feeling just that little bit more protected. She sticks with light.

She settles back down a little while later, resting her head on the pillow and is back in her fetal position with a pillow between her knees for support. Her heart has relaxed a bit but the aftereffects of adrenaline are still lingering. She feels a bit jittery and uneasy, but tries to get some sleep.

Seconds later, Charlie's senses registered that something is touching her arm. For a split nanosecond she thinks that Everett has come home early but it is not Everett. There is a one-fingered hand coming into view and then the wrist and finally a black-sleeved arm comes around her shoulder and is starting to squeeze her like a boa constrictor. Charlie begins to flail her arms and thrash her body to escape her captor.

Panic sets in, but she is entangled in the sheets and blanket, she cannot free herself. She is screaming but there is no one to hear her screams. The arm is so tight around her pulling her off the bed. Charlie finally manages to at least turn to face her attacker and there is no one there. No arm or person to whom an arm should be attached to.

*Starting Again*

Her eyes register that there is no one there but she is overtaken by a feeling as if her body is being possessed by an evil spirit. It feels like an internal vibration but the vibrations are being caused by electricity. Every fiber, muscle, and inch of skin is vibrating. She is screaming but she can't hear herself so either she is not screaming or she has gone deaf. She shuts her eyes so tight, as tight as she can, to make everything stop or go away or get out of her.

She is suddenly paralyzed and can't move or open her eyes. She doesn't feel the arm any longer, but it feels like the whole room is now vibrating at the same rhythm as what is going on inside her. She is scared and wants it to all stop. "Please stop please stop please stop," she keeps repeating to herself. Finally, slowly, the unwanted feelings leave her body and she gains control. She opens her eyes and sees nothing out of place.

Charlie immediately checks that her belly is still there and checks for blood in the sheets. Belly is still there and no blood, so the baby seems okay. "What the fuck was that?" she says out loud to no one but herself. She starts to register that the music is playing and recognizes the song. Slowly, the thumping in her ears ceases. She is covered in sweat. As the fear and the adrenaline are being replaced in her body a wave a sadness comes over her and she cannot control or stop it. She sobs into her hands. She wants Everett to be home right now.

Eventually, life returns to normal. Charlie is shocked that it is one in the morning. She must have fallen asleep and that was a vivid dream. Vivid feels like an understatement, since she could feel the arm squeezing her and pulling her. A one-fingered arm no less, floating and not attached to a body. Charlie talks it out in her mind, rationalizing it was a bad dream, and she is safe.

Charlie changes the sheets and her pj's. She pushes the bed from the middle of the room to the closest wall so that no one or nothing can come up behind her when she is lying on her side again. The bed moves easily on the hardwood floors, so not a big task for Charlie in her pregnant state.

Charlie crawls back into bed, seeking out that sweet spot she had found earlier. Having her back to the wall gives her some consolation and within a half hour she feels warm and safe. Maybe she will get some good rest tonight, she hopes. Charlie focuses again on the music, her eyes are closed. She is tapping her toes to the beat of the music. She looks at the clock on the windowsill, and reads 11:11. Her favorite number. Charlie smiles and then as if her brain had a conversation without her and then clued her in on the question it came up with, wasn't it one a.m. not that long ago? Is time going backwards?

As she finished that thought, she felt something tugging on her socks. It is not a gentle tugging and her socks were being pulled off her feet. She looked down to see a woman; she is young with her hair braided, big gold loop earrings, and a light sports jacket that reflected in the hallway light. Charlie screamed for real this time, out loud and loudly.

"Who are you and what are you doing? Get off me!" she says, kicking her feet at the grabbing hands. "Get off me and get out of my house." She tries thrashing once again to get free. The stranger manages to pull off Charlie's socks and is now working on Charlie pj pants.

"You have so much, and we need it to stay warm in the winter. We have children and elderly people suffering. You can afford it," the young woman says as she stops pulling on Charlie's clothing but stands her ground at the foot of the bed with her arms folded now across her chest. "We have nothing and you have so much."

*The woman is right*, thought Charlie, *I do have so much*. So she got out of bed and took all her clothing off and gave them to her. Charlie emptied her closet of the warmest of her clothing and gave those to the strange woman in her room in the middle of the night. *Evil always comes out at nighttime*, Charlie thinks to herself.

## *Starting Again*

Charlie finds herself back in bed without remembering how she got there, and the same low-intensity vibrations takes over her body again. Her eyes squeeze shut involuntarily and she is paralyzed. It feels like the whole world is vibrating, like crossing into another universe. It eventually releases its grip on Charlie and the vibrations disappear and she can open her eyes again. She regains full mobility. She blinks and looks at the foot of her bed and she is alone.

Charlie feels completely alone and scared and now she is either being haunted or having night terrors. Or seizures, it could be anything, and she is worried about the baby now. Is this related to the pregnancy? Is this normal? None of the books she read ever mentioned having episodes like this. Charlie really wished Everett was here to console her and lend a theory that would make her feel better.

It is now three in the morning, only three hours left until she is due to wake up anyway. Charlie absolutely knows deep in her bones that she won't be sleeping in the house for three hours, so she gets up and bakes two apple pies. Hopefully Everett will be home soon.

# Chapter 34

## Everett

The night is the worst. The day was all right because I was distracted and busy finding new places and grabbing what supplies I could. The bigger cities proved to be very bountiful and worth the trip. I found food and new places to go. No stores were being run so nothing new seems to have been brought in, but electricity is still working so frozen and canned products are still good.

I found a generator and stocked up on as much gas as I could in the canisters I found. More baby stuff than we could possibly ever use, medical supplies, gardening supplies. It is a good trip. It is almost worth being away from Charlie. Almost.

It is strange to be in a large city that was once bustling with people, tourists, and the homeless. Now so quiet you can hear the powerlines buzz in the middle of the day. I half expected to see other humans, but not one, not even a trace of one.

I am sleeping in a trailer camper van I found. I hooked it up to the truck and hooked the trailer to the van. It will be a slow drive home but it has other sources of power like propane that could be useful during storms. I think to myself I will give it a go, driving it all hooked up as it is, and if it doesn't work out I'll leave it behind. Come back another day to get it.

I am warm and enjoying a microwave meal early; comfy and cozy in the sleeping area with my sleeping bag that I also found. But all I can think of is Charlie now, in the darkness of the night. I am exhausted and would like to sleep, but feel disconnected from her. I feel alone. I am worried about her. I don't think I could drive much or safely especially with the configuration going on behind the truck. I don't know what to do. I struggle to make a decision. If Charlie was with me she would help me to calm down, refocus, and chat out the options.

Either I try to sleep and my attempt will be successful or not. If it is not, driving back would be a much more valuable use of my time. If I do sleep I will be more alert and a better driver. By the time I finish my internal debate on what to do it is about three in the morning. *Ah, fuck it*, I say to myself, *let's drive back*. I can sleep once I know Charlie is okay.

I get out of bed, get dressed, and head out of the camper van and into the truck. I am parked just on the edge of town, easy access to the highway. So I start my journey home, I am about two hours away so will make it just before Charlie wakes up.

When I pull onto the highway a flash of white runs across my side of the highway but is blocked by the barriers that separate the two sides. As I pass where the flash stopped at the barriers, I look as I drive by and notice it is a furry ball huddled against the cement barriers.

"What the . . ." I say and I pull over. I have to be honest, driving is so much better when you are alone on the road. The stop and pull over is slow as I can't just jam on my brakes, but eventually

## Starting Again

I do come to a full stop about fifteen feet away. I get out of my truck and start hoofing it. I'm pretty sure it is an animal, so I am prepared to help it back to safety off the highway. I don't think I hit it so not expecting blood and gore.

The white ball is getting closer, not moving or running away. It actually looks like it is coming towards me. It is dark and hard to tell what it is until it is right in front of me. Standing there is a white-furred puppy. It's wagging its tail at me and then starts to jump up on my legs like it wants me to pick it up.

I haven't seen any free-roaming animals in any of my trips away from home. I had fully intended to adopt any cows or horses or chickens from neighbors or anywhere we had gone, but none. None, not a one. Not even dead bodies, which I half expected as they heartbreakingly die of starvation.

And here stands this very young puppy who had to have been born in nature, staring at me. Pleading for help. I don't really ponder for very long, of course I'll bring it home with me and take care of it. I have always wanted a dog but it was never an option either as a child or as an adult. I feel very giddy as I pick it up and bring it close to my face for inspection. Looks healthy enough, no mange or visible signs of malnourishment.

I take a look around to make sure there aren't brother or sisters or a mama looking for this one, and when I don't find any, I head back to the truck. I wonder how Charlie will feel about a dog. She loves all the other animals, so I don't think she will oppose. And what else can we do? I'm not going to leave it here to an uncertain and bleak future.

I take a look at the undercarriage and discover we have a she, and I let her get cozy in my sweater on the passenger seat. She instantly falls asleep as soon as the truck is grumbling and moving. Poor thing probably hasn't had a solid sleep in a while, well, at least since she lost her mom and family.

As we are driving I remember that on my way in I saw a big garden center just on the outskirts. Those stores usually have dog supplies. I get off at the next exit and as luck would have it, I am right, and manage to find it fairly easily. Once in the parking lot I can see lights on inside so I scoop up the puppy, tuck her into my jacket to free my hands, and head for the door.

It is open and, score two for me, there are pet supplies. I grab a flatbed trolly and start stacking bags of food, toys, collars, jackets, leashes, a crate, bath care products, and a couple of beds. We are in and out in a matter of thirty minutes, back on the road. I should make it home now by the time Charlie is waking up. I'll have a breakfast surprise for her.

# Chapter 35

## Together

Charlie hears the truck wheels crunching on the gravel before she sees the truck. Joy takes over every inch of her body, Everett is home and so early. Charlie had been keeping busy in the kitchen for the last three hours. She looks like the old Rice Krispies commercial, where the mom flicks some flour in her face to make it look like she's been in the kitchen working hard, Charlie has flour all over her face, in her hair, and on her housecoat.

It is still dark out, it is only six a.m., but Charlie can see the headlights winding down the driveway. If it wasn't still dark and full of evil demons outside, and one degree, she would fly out the door and throw herself at him. Wrap her arms as far around him as she could considering her lovely baby bump and the two lovely lady humps that come with the bump.

So she waits patiently at the door for him. The truck is moving slow and there are shadows way long behind it, but Charlie is too focused on watching the driver. She can see him as he opens the door and the inside light comes on. His jacket is puffed out and he is holding his stomach. Charlie instantly starts sweating. Did he hurt himself?

He is barely at the door before Charlie flings it open abruptly and takes the three steps to reach him. Charlie spreads her arms like an eagle soaring in the sky to envelop Everett in her embrace, but Everett takes a step back and extends the non-stomach holding arm out to stop her. Her smile slowly slides off her face but Charlie notices that Everett's is big and wide.

"Wait, I don't want our precious cargos to collide," he says and gives her a mischievous wink. Charlie is unsure of what is going on as she watches him unzip his jacket and stuff a hand in there. Everett slowly pulls out the puppy from his jacket and holds her in front of Charlie like the lion king. "I found a puppy!"

Charlie is filled with relief Everett is not hurt, content that Everett is home, exhaustion from not sleeping and still growing a baby, and giddiness from the cute little fur ball in Everett's hands. Everett hands the puppy to Charlie. The puppy is wagging her little white tail and licking her chin in equal dog giddiness.

Everett is happy that Charlie seems to be okay with him bringing home another girl, furry as she is, but also notices that Charlie looks haggard, like she aged by ten years over the last two days. She has dark circles under her eyes, she seems to have wrinkles around her eyes as well that he doesn't remember being there when he left. Maybe it is just the lighting and the fact she is covered in flour.

"Why you up, and why are you covered in flour?"

"Come inside, there is a pie cooling. We will sit and have breakfast," Charlie replies, but only half paying attention. The other half is focused on the puppy and cooing and awing at her. Charlie turns on a dime and marches back inside the house.

## Starting Again

"What are we going to name it, is it a boy or a girl?" Charlie asks, more to the universe than Everett, flipping the puppy over to take a look and find out the sex. "Oh, a girl, it's a girl!"

"I am playing around with Shadow, what do you think?" Everett says, but he almost whispers the name, unsure how Charlie will take to it. He really likes it and has always wanted a dog and to name it Shadow.

"Shadow, do you look like a Shadow? Let's see. Shadow, come here, girl." Charlie is using a low, sweet voice as she calls the puppy she had put down nanoseconds ago. The puppy is sniffing around on the ground, but as soon as Charlie called her she perked her head up, ears and all, and looked right at Charlie. "I guess Shadow it is!"

Everett's insides do a little flip. The nine-year-old boy inside him gives forty-year-old him a high five. "Oh, I missed you. Ignore that dog for a second and come here." He pulls Charlie to him by her housecoat and spins her by the waist so that she is facing him. Everett lands his lips on hers, lingers and takes in her warm, soft breath.

After a minute or so, they part lips but their faces are still close together. Charlie kisses Everett on the chin, and the cheeks and the tip of his nose with tender caring love. "You are never leaving me ever again. I go where you go. I don't care if we have to bring all the dumb animals with us."

"Deal, I feel the same. Never again. But it was a good trip. I did most of the mid-island to the bottom tip. There was way more out there than I thought and we have supplies for a bit. I will go get the frozen food and cans after we eat. Animal feed, medical supplies, gardening supplies. You name it, I got it. I got more baby stuff. And picked up this little hitchhiker along the way."

Charlie is cutting one of the two pies she baked into slices, and scooping one out for Everett. "That's great, we will have a busy day getting it all unloaded. I'll feed the animals, including this little

*203*

hitchhiker and then come help you." The word *you* came out of Charlie's mouth with a deep yawn.

"Are you okay, how did you sleep?" Everett barely got out as he shoved another forkful of pie into his drooling mouth.

"I've had better. I had nightmares all night, well, they felt real and vivid all night. It was weird as they both ended with me feeling paralyzed and shutting my eyes involuntarily. That's why I'm up and there are baked pies. Decided to get up and face my demons one apple at a time." Charlie gave a little chuckle but that quickly turned into another yawn.

"Babe, that sounds horrible. Has the baby moved in a while?" Everett didn't want to seem insensitive but also didn't want to sound alarmed. That sounded a bit like a seizure and he is worried about Mom but also mostly baby.

"While I was baking the baby was moving all about doing the hokey pokey." Shadow, who had been sniffing around her new home, had made her way back to her humans and is asking for Charlie to pick her up. She's now nuzzling into Charlie's neck with her stinky puppy breath.

"If it happens again you wake me up, okay? Let's hope it doesn't happen again. You want to go lie down? I'm good to do chores and empty the truck and trailer." Everett didn't want to do it all alone as he felt equally tired, but Charlie could use some rest.

"No, I am okay. I want to try to force myself and go to bed early. I'll check in if I need some rest. Promise."

It is close to seven a.m. before they are dressed, fed, and out the door. Not knowing what kind of breed Shadow is, Charlie is a bit hesitant to let her out without a leash, but she seemed to stay very close to Charlie the whole time. Shadow liked the animals and all the smells; she rolled in the hay and chased the barn cat. Charlie stopped a few times to watch Shadow and all her goofy characteristics. She seems to have fit into the family just like that.

# Chapter 36

## Together

Christmas is just around the corner, only five days away, and the festive season spirits fill the Wolfe and Peterson household. It turns out that both Everett and Charlie love Christmas, it is their favorite holiday. They decorate the house and the barn with evergreens, lights, and balls. Charlie's belly is a ball itself. She is carrying a watermelon at this point, and Everett has caught her waddling when she walks. So things are getting ready, less than two months left.

The baby room is all done up. Everett surprised Charlie shortly after he came back from his overnight supply run by putting the crib up, painting, and adding a few decorations. Mostly toys and books but it looks really cute. Charlie needs to rest more these days so is able to sneak it in while she napped. The room is a pretty yellow, a great color for either a boy or girl.

Their afternoon cuddles are usually now spent feeling the baby move, well, more watching the baby move. Shadow has even learnt to come in and stay quiet, laying awkwardly on top of their feet. Their little family has already expanded.

Shadow has settled into the family quite seamlessly; she doesn't run away but is a total puppy. Besides the annoying puppy behaviors of biting everything with her piranha teeth and being full of energy, which Charlie is not, she is a very good dog. She sleeps great on her cushion beside the bed, super easygoing about food, and has imprinted onto Everett. She will follow Charlie around, but Everett is her human.

They brought in an evergreen tree the other day and decorated that, there are even some presents under it already. They had done what any couple would have done during the holiday season, split up while shopping and no snooping. There will be some things for Shadow, too: new toys. Things are merry and bright at the Wolfe-Peterson household.

Charlie is in the kitchen making some gingerbread cookies to decorate, to eat, and use in the tree as decorations. Everett is helping with the decorating, humming a Christmas tune as he worked. Charlie couldn't imagine a better life, watching Everett wearing a big smile, rubbing her belly. Even Shadow running around the house with socks she found in the laundry room fit in her perfect family moment vision.

"So what are we going to name this kid already? I'm happy to wait to see what the baby looks like for a first name when he or she comes out, but what about a last name? Are we going to be those parents that give tons of middle names and hyphen the last name?" Charlie asks, which breaks Everett's focus on adding colored buttons to the gingerbread person he is working on.

Everett doesn't have any middle names and isn't really fussy either way about that. He never really put much thought into a last name, there won't be a birth certificate or school to worry about. He pondered for a few seconds.

"Why don't we all, all three of us, become Wolfe-Peterson? We are a family and the baby is half you and half me." Seemed like a simple solution, but, again, Everett is happy with whatever Charlie wanted.

"I love that, it is us." Charlie couldn't help the feelings welling in her heart come out as tears. They were tears of happiness but tears nonetheless.

And, in turn, Charlie's tears of happiness were enough for Everett to feel closely connected to Charlie even more than he already felt. Everett isn't sure if it is because it is Christmas or the baby is going to be born soon, or what, but he is a bit more emotional. He missed his family and his traditions, and he knew he had a new family and would make new traditions, but it just seemed to hit home more during the holidays.

Charlie wiped her face with her apron, which is covered in flour leaving flour streaks on her cheeks. Like war paint. Or like she is going hunting, in camouflage. Something about the wholesomeness of that action caught Everett's eye. Charlie is standing with her side facing Everett, her belly is big now but her silhouette is still slender and beautiful. She is wearing a one-piece bodysuit under the apron. Hugging her curves in all the right places.

Everett is sitting and could feel his pants getting tight as he followed the lines of her body starting from her legs, up to her butt, to the soft curve at her lumbar area and all around her full pregnant breast. The apron may have protected her body from flour but it is not doing any protecting from his eyes.

Charlie caught Everett's eyes doing a once-over, making her feel very sexy despite feeling very heavy at the moment. They still had sex, how could they not with Everett looking the way he does and loving her the way he does. But she had not seen lust in his eyes since *50 Shades of Grey* happened a while back. Lust had been replaced with love and tenderness. This look is neither, and Charlie liked it, replacing her feelings of deep-rooted happiness with an animallike urge. Everett could almost sense that urge in Charlie, feel it in the air. The hairs on his arms stood up with anticipation.

Charlie, still standing, slowly took off her apron and let her hair down. Never breaking eye contact. She turned around so that her back is facing Everett, looked over her shoulder with a sly smile, and gave Everett a cheeky wink. From behind you would never be able to tell she is pregnant.

Everett almost growled out loud when she looked back at him. As he watched her ever so slowly slide her bodysuit off her shoulders and arms, one at a time. When she tugged the material gently over her breasts, Everett could see the bounce as they rebounded back into place. Everett is no longer semi erect but fully, pushing up against the material of his jeans.

Charlie continued to move the bodysuit down along her back and over her tummy. Bending over is no short feat at this stage of her pregnancy, so Everett would have to do the rest for her once she got to under her belly. But before turning she started swaying her hips to music only in her mind. Wrapping her hands around her own upper body, Everett could only see her hands moving up and down her naked back.

Charlie swayed and dipped as far as she could, slowly moving back to a standing position. Moving her hands in the same rhythm. Everett could no longer take not touching her, he stood with such vigor that the chair he is sitting on toppled over. The noise broke Charlie's trance in her dance, startled her a little. But by the time she jumped, Everett is already behind her. His body is pressed up against hers, she could feel his hard-on in her lower back.

Everett cupped her breasts, which overflowed out of his hands now, catching Charlie's breath. Everett massaged and squeezed the flesh in his hands, feeling her nipples harden in his palms. Charlie's head leaned back onto Everett's chest, exposing her throat. Without thinking, Everett brought one of his hands up

## Starting Again

to her throat and wrapped his fingers around it. Not putting any pressure, just holding it firmly.

Charlie's knees gave out a little in reaction to his firmness, around her throat and pressed against her back. Everett spoke into Charlie's ear with authority to not move, and proceeded to remove the bodysuit all the way down her sexy body. His fingers tracing the curves of her legs as he stood up, allowing them to take a sharp right turn at her hips to find her clit to give her a little pleasure.

Charlie moaned with each stroke, spread her legs unconsciously little by little. Charlie spun to face Everett and tore at his clothes, barely having the first item fully removed before hurriedly moving on to the next one.

Everett, now fully naked, pressed Charlie to his body and picked her up by her bum. Using his body as a support and guide to get her to sit on the floured counter, Charlie is surprised at how light she felt, or how light Everett made her feel when he picked her up. He buried his face in her cleavage, kissing and nibbling her warm and soft flesh. He could feel her heartbeat, it is racing with anticipation.

Everett took Charlie's face in his hands and looked her dead in the eyes, and without breaking eye contact pulled her legs to move her bottom just off the edge of the counter and entered her. The angle isn't satisfactory for Everett, and Charlie isn't a fan of it either. "Wrap your legs around my waist," he demanded.

"I'm too heavy, I'll hurt you," Charlie countered.

"I can carry a calf and I can carry you. You weigh half their weight."

Charlie reluctantly did as she is instructed, and is not sure why she doubted Everett, he carried her around like she is a backpack on the front of his body. Pushing off his hips with her thighs, Charlie started moving up and down so that he would enter her and exit, just not all the way. Wash, rinse, repeat. Up, down, and repeat. Everett is lost in her breasts and the moment, she felt good around him and on him.

The belly is also making this position a bit more challenging, not that it didn't feel good, but it threw Charlie off her rhythm. So she released her legs to dismount Everett. Everett pulled out, allowing her to go down and supporting her as she went. Charlie turned around and braced herself up against the dining table. Bending down slightly, presenting Everett with her willing, wanting love clam.

Everett always felt more in control when he entered from behind. Not in her behind, just that position. As if dominating her. It isn't the dominating part, but he could control her movements and controlled how fast he came.

What Charlie is presenting him looked tasty and he kneeled down to take a quick lick before standing and guiding his erection into her. Charlie is wet, didn't need much lubrication. Everett could tell she is very aroused and he is close. Rocking in and out of Charlie felt so good, each stroke brings him closer and closer to the ultimate release.

Charlie could feel Everett's thumb adding just a little pressure on her butt hole, never going in more than a thumbprint. Different stimulation but just as good. Everett adjusted his tactics and pushed his thumb down and up at the same time as he entered and pulled out of her. Keeping that pace going knocked Charlie's socks off, and she was caught off guard with how fast and intense her orgasm came on and exploded.

"Oh my gawd, oh my gawd, I'm coming. It's coming, don't stop. Everett, Everett," Charlie belted out as she came. Everett waited until she had finished experiencing her orgasm, and started to pump a bit hard and deeper. Charlie is still tight and she surrounded him fully. Everett let his orgasm overcome him and with a final grunt of satisfaction, laying limp on top of Charlie who is laying limp on the table covered in cookies.

*Starting Again*

Shadow had gone to sleep in her little doggie bed in the corner of the kitchen during the whole event.

# Chapter 37

## Together

Christmas and New Year came and went, it was lovely and special. They created their own traditions and couldn't wait until the baby was born to partake in their family traditions. It had snowed for a couple of weeks, and Charlie thought the scenery was so beautiful, as if the clouds had sprinkled icing sugar over Vancouver Island. The snow was a unique event, making it special even if the cold made chores less fun.

Everett seemed to be thriving with their routines and schedules, Everett forgets less, closes cupboards, picks up the bath mat. Or maybe Charlie is just doing more. With a month to go, she seemed to be nesting. Cleaning and preparing for the baby. With the canning and preserving all done until the fall, Charlie filled her time with getting ready as best she could.

Everett is preparing as well, but he is more internally and Charlie is externally. He is worrying and planning for the birth and aftercare. The baby is moving so much and you could see a hand or foot pressing against Charlie's tummy. With the movements so visible there is no point in doing any ultrasounds and they haven't really done any for a month or so.

The birth is really freaking Everett out so he prepared as best he could, with research and multiple plans for every scenario he could think of. Although the planning helped, it also meant his brain is on hyperdrive day in and day out. Everett isn't sleeping a whole lot despite being tired.

Tonight he hopped on his stationary bike to burn off some energy and give his brain a break. Charlie is busy with putting the baby clothing in the drawers and stacking diapers. Charlie hummed songs that came into her head as she busied around the room, Shadow following her around. Shadow is not a fan of when Everett is on the bike, she kept nipping at his heels as if trying to save him from the big scary beast. She learned to just seek out Charlie or seek out trouble. Seeking out Charlie resulted in more treats than stern looks.

They were in different rooms but they each could hear the other in what they were doing. Charlie could hear the hum of the bike and Everett could hear Charlie closing drawers. It has become part of the background noise for both of them. Conscious and unconscious in the same drop. Everett pedaled faster and faster, trying to quiet his mind just for a few minutes. With only a month left those moments were few and far between.

He is lost in thought, thinking about what it would be like to have a baby in their lives. Charlie and he had not known each other very long but they had built a strong relationship, a strong bond to each other. He wondered how having another person would impact that relationship. That, too, worried him. He had guilty thoughts that he is not ready or able to share to Charlie even if that is with his own flesh and blood.

Everett shook his head, as if trying to shake the shameful thought out of his mind and out his ear. He pedaled on, he only had

## *Starting Again*

a few more minutes left. He focused on the hum of the machine, the creaks of the house, the rain outside hitting the windows. Like an electric shock to his system he realized he hadn't heard any noise from the room where Charlie was.

He stopped pedaling but the noise from the equipment needed a few seconds to power down. He paused, still as a deer caught in headlights. No sound. "Charlie, you okay?" Everett stayed as still as could be to better hear the slightest peep. Charlie did not reply nor did he hear her hum or sing or sneeze. No furniture being closed or moved around.

Everett's skin tingled and without consciously thinking about it he is unclipped and off the bike, moving quickly to the baby's room. "Babe, you okay? Everything okay?" As the last word left his lips he turned the corner to the room and found Charlie sitting in the rocking chair, bent over, clasping her belly.

Everett propelled himself at Charlie, at her feet. "What's wrong? Charlie talk to me, what's wrong?"

"I'm cramping, or it is contractions. It just came on all of a sudden," Charlie managed to say before another wave hit and she clenched her teeth and bared down.

"Did your water break or did you lose the mucus plug?" Everett asks in his assessment. He speaks as he takes her vitals.

"No," is all Charlie could get out.

"Okay, anything feel out of the ordinary? We read a bunch of books on childbirth, so anything outside those symptoms?"

"No, just cramping in my belly." The cramp has subsided so Charlie is able to sit a bit straighter and get a few extra words out.

"And now, no pain?" Everett said as he looked at his watch to note the time in the event that this is it.

"Still pain but less intense, my muscles are more relaxed."

"Okay, don't move. Sorry, stupid thing to say, but I'll be right back." Everett is gone and back in a flash with a blood pressure

215

cuff, stethoscope, and a piece of paper. "I'm just going to check on your blood pressure and note down when the cramping stopped."

Everett worked quickly and efficiently. You could tell this is not his first time taking someone's blood pressure. A minute passed and he removed the cuff. "All good, 120 over 80."

Charlie nodded her head while bending over again to ride out another wave of cramping and pain. She squeezed the end of the armrest of the rocking chair as she made a growly groan noise. Everett stood up and rubbed Charlie's back hoping that helped relieve the pain a bit, looking at his watch to time how long this one lasted. He isn't convinced it is contractions but the alternatives weren't good so he focused on what he could control.

This went on just long enough that Everett is almost convinced Charlie was in labor, but it did end about half an hour later. The longest half an hour of his life, but it has been two hours now and no more cramping. The baby is moving and there is no bleeding, so Everett is hoping it is only something he had read about called Braxton Hicks, which is false labor. This could mean the real thing is coming soon or could still be a while.

That night Everett still didn't sleep but for different reasons. He is watching Charlie, waiting to see if more cramps were coming or if labor would start. He had thought about that moment for the last three months, what it would be like when labor starts.

His favorite scenario is they both have had a good night's sleep, had breakfast and labor starts then. Charlie stands up from the kitchen dining table and her water breaks. Things run smoothly and baby is born healthy. He has prepared himself for a variety of scenarios, many are his least favorite. He is prepared to do a C-section if needed, but he is really hoping that that scenario doesn't happen.

Everett watches Charlie's chest go up and down as she breathes. He catches the little track runner in her stomach move a few times. He watches her move and tries to stay out of her way when she

## Starting Again

looks comfortable. Tonight was a bit scary but mostly he is wide awake because it is real now. This baby is coming and he has no control on how. He loves Charlie and this is so far out of his realm and he has had so much time to ponder and focus on the worst-case scenario. His job has prepared him for the emergency part of life. This is way too much prep.

Around three a.m. he gets out of bed, careful not to wake Charlie, and goes to the kitchen to get something to drink. As he stands at the sink, glass in hand and tap running, Everett's heart rate spikes. He is instantly sweating and he wants to rip his skin suit off. He cannot stand being confined by his skin a minute longer. He is getting dizzy and starts to cry uncontrollably. He can't catch his breath. He claws at his chest, it felt like a cow is sitting there and he needs to move it.

Everett sits on the ground because he feels like he is going to lose consciousness. The floor is freezing cold against the skin of his legs. The fire has died and it is the middle of winter and the night. The shock of the cold floor seems to reboot his system. He can breathe again and his heart rate is slowing down. "What the fuck was that!"

"Are you okay?" a groggy, low voice says from behind Everett. Everett looks up to see Charlie waddling towards him, rubbing her eyes, shielding them from the light as her sight adjusts. "What happened, why are you on the floor?" Charlie is asking questions faster than he can answer them.

"I'm okay. I just couldn't breathe and my heart rate exploded."

"Sounds like a panic attack. I read about them in a book. How are you feeling now?"

"Better. I'm sorry if I woke you up. I was actually trying to let you sleep."

"You know I don't sleep well when you are not there, now come back to bed. I'll run my hands through your hair like you like."

"You don't need to do that, you need your sleep. I'll go to the couch."

Charlie would have none of the nonsense, and Everett gave in and they both headed back to bed. To Everett's surprise he fell asleep pretty quickly, Charlie had that effect on him. And he slept all the way to seven a.m., and woke up with the worst headache he has ever had.

# Chapter 38

## Charlie

It could be any day now, it is February 10 and tomorrow would be the exact due date. I am hoping for tomorrow, since eleven is my favorite number. But I have zero control over this so we will go about our day as normal. It could be a couple of weeks more, who knows. We are both anxious and scared and excited.

Shadow senses our feelings. Even as a little puppy she is clingier and never wanders far. She is the cutest dog and we both hope she will adjust well to having the baby around. If you had asked me a year ago where I would be on this date, married and about to have a baby, living and thriving on a cute little farm with a dog and tons of animals would not have been my answer.

If you had asked me ten years ago I would have said drunk or dead somewhere, because even though I knew I was going down a dark path with alcohol, I couldn't stop. I was voluntarily killing myself. Now I am sober, happy, and fulfilled. I know that our future is uncertain, and most likely won't be this calm and free, but for right now this is paradise if you ask me.

Everett is amazing and I have no idea what I did to find him, and build this all with him. He is kind and loving, thoughtful and sexy as hell. I don't care that he is forgetful or struggles with ADD; that is what I diagnosed him with from my many nights reading. He loves me and I feel important to him. It is good to feel important to someone, especially if you have lost all your friends and family. We will heal together.

Everett, Shadow, and this baby are my family now, and I am grateful every day. When I was diagnosed with cancer, which was my biggest fear as an alcoholic, I didn't feel I deserved any happiness for all the bad decisions, the shit I caused. To others and myself. How I disrespected my body and all that time I could have been living instead of drinking. Some days I still don't feel like I deserve to feel as happy as I do. But I do, truly do. I wake up every morning grateful for another day to live and love.

It is just after lunch, and we are taking a bit of a rest. Everett from working all morning and me from just simply being a humongous baby maker. I have my tea, hot and steamy in my hands. Warming my soul starting at my fingers. I am staring outside from my perch on the couch. Shadow is lying next to me and on the other side is Everett reading.

I find the rain and dark clouds today stunning. All the shades of gray and white, and the rain making everything shiny. You would think the rain would make me sad but it doesn't. Everything and everyone needs water, to me water is life.

I have a ceramic mug that says, "*Yes I talk to myself, sometimes I need expert advice.*" It makes me laugh each time I read it. I bring the mug to my mouth to take a sip and the baby moves at the same time. Lately this baby likes to get stuck under my ribs, making sitting down bitterly uncomfortable. I put a hand on my stomach to connect with the baby and to coax it down. The baby moves

## *Starting Again*

again but this time a sharp pain that starts from my pubic area and shoots up my belly follows the movement.

"Ouch." I put the mug down.

"Are you okay?" Everett looks at me and asks with a hint of concern on his face. I can tell he doesn't want to overreact but, like I said, any moment.

"Sharp pain, not sure if the baby pushed on something. I'm fine." All of a sudden I feel wet between my legs, drenched is a better word for it. "Oh shit, did I pee myself?" I'm shocked that I did that, I didn't feel like I needed to pee.

"I don't think that is pee, I think your water just broke." Everett jumps up nearly bouncing me off the couch, and scared Shadow to the next room.

A pain plus the feeling as if someone is wrapping an elastic bandage wrap around my belly starts. The pain isn't bad, more like a poop cramp. This is it, that must have been a contraction. I tell Everett when it ended so we can count how long and how quick they come on. It could be hours or even days before this baby comes out. I am prepared to do what is needed to bring our little miracle into the world.

Everett and I have talked about what to try, positions and techniques to help with the pain and stack the odds of a safe delivery in our corner. We know that there are a variety of ways this could go and we will just have to go with the flow since this baby is being born outside of a hospital with no medical staff to care for us.

Everett is outwardly calm, but I'm sure he is a bag of jitters inside. But he is methodically checking things off the list and making sure I am comfortable at the same time. He has brought me the yoga ball to sit on, he has helped me change into a muumuu for easy access. I trust my life and the life of this baby a hundred percent in Everett's hands. I feel it in my bones that we can do this.

The labor is slow and low intensity for about four hours, this is when I lose my mucus plug. Just looked like a big snot but it didn't

*221*

come from my nose. The contractions are about fifteen minutes apart still and last about a minute. Everett is rubbing my back, my feet, my hair, whatever he thinks will make me more comfortable. I've walked a little, rolled on the yoga ball a little bit, and sat down a little bit. I know this will get worse but feel ignorantly optimistic that I've got this.

It is around six p.m. now, and I have told Everett to go eat. He needs to keep his strength up just as much as me. I am sitting on the ground, quietly in a comfy position, grounding myself when I can feel a contraction coming on. This time it is more painful and it now feels like my stomach muscles are being pulled apart but towards the back. This one makes me sweat a little.

"Just had another one, this one is a bit more painful," I scream out to Everett who is down the hallway having something to eat quickly in the kitchen.

"Copy that," Everett screams back with a mouth full of something. I hear his footsteps coming down the hallway a nanosecond later.

"Let's check to see how dilated you are. I've never done this but read it is easy enough to tell with fingers. My hands are clean and warm." Everett gives me a soft, endearing smile. I'm not hugely excited for him to be looking down there in this capacity but he's all I've got so I hoist myself up off the floor and lay down on the bed in the baby's room. It is a spare mattress so we will be throwing it out after this I'm sure.

I spread my legs and Everett disappears under my muumuu. "Isn't this how we got into this predicament in the first place?" I giggle. I still have energy and my wits about me so I thought I would throw out a joke. Everett peaks up from under my hospital gown-like dress, gives me a mischievous grin, and heads back in. I can feel his finger go in but it is not painful or pleasurable, it is just what it is.

"I think everything is good. You are dilated but I can't tell how much. We will check in periodically as needed." He just barely finished his sentence when a contraction hit me, it is a big one, biggest yet. I felt like someone with giant hands is squeezing my stomach. I had to breathe this one out and grind my teeth a little.

"I'm getting scared, this is getting way more intense and I don't think I'm close to pushing. It is just going to get more painful each time," I manage to say when the contraction passes, and as Everett is wiping my forehead with a cool cloth.

"You are a strong badass of a woman, and I'm so in awe of how amazing you are. I'm here every step of the way. I know you can do this."

His words of encouragement were sweet and came from a good place but he isn't pushing this baby out. I decided to get up and walk around, Everett joined me and put his arm around my waist. Okay, he might not be pushing this baby out but he will be with me every step of the way. Tears fill my eyes, gratefulness overwhelms me. "Are you having another contraction?" Everett wipes my tears away and squeezes me closer to his body. His strong, caring body.

"No. I just love you so much and I couldn't have imagined a better person to share my life with. Thank you for being you."

Everett seemed touched as his eyes welled up, which kept mine tearing. We were a hot mess at this very moment. But ain't nobody got time for feelings, another contraction was coming. "Another one is coming." I braced myself against Everett and rode out the wave. "They are getting more painful."

"That one was seven minutes from the last one. They are getting closer. You are doing great." Everett kissed the top of my head and walked me to the living room to take my blood pressure again. "Everything looks great. And in case you didn't know, I love you, too, so much. You are my forever."

# Chapter 39

# Together

Another five hours passed. Everett looked at the clock which read ten thirty p.m. The contractions slowly went from seven minutes apart to five minutes apart to this point. Charlie worked hard, harder than anything in her life to bring this baby into the world. With every passing hour the contractions intensified. Charlie screamed in pain, braced herself, squeezed, walked, hunched, rolled, and went on all fours.

Everett never left Charlie's side, not even to pee. At ten thirty Everett confirmed via another check that Charlie is at ten centimeters, if not close to. He is no doctor but she had progressed to approximately the size of a baby's head. This is good because Charlie is ready to push through the pain. And not just figuratively but literally.

"I think it is time to push, does it feel right to push?" Everett asked, brushing her wet, sweaty hair out of her face.

"Yep, yes it does. I want to push. I want to push so bad," she breathed out. She is a little out of breath from recovering from the contractions. "Everett, I read I could shit while I push. Please still love me if I do."

Everett smiled and tilted his head. "I've seen worse I'm sure, shit doesn't scare me. Nothing could stop me from loving you."

Charlie nodded her head and grabbed her legs from behind her knees. She is lying down now as it is the more comfortable position at this point in her labor. Charlie is ready, not ready for an hour and a half of active labor but she had heard worse stories. She pushed and absorbed the pain to push again. Everett is encouraging her from his place between her legs.

"I can see the head, Charlie, I can see the top of the head. You are amazing, I can see our baby!"

Charlie is breathing out the pain but managed a nod. Shadow had not been in the way at all, she kept her distance but is never too far that she didn't have a clear line of sight. She whimpered once or twice during the worst of the contractions. She is calming to Charlie, just to see her made things a smidge better.

Charlie's whole body felt like she had run a marathon but then was hit by a bus, after which a semi-truck rolled over her. She is exhausted and didn't feel she could keep going, but somehow found the strength to keep pushing. She could feel parts moving through her, slow at first but then all of a sudden a swoosh and it felt like the baby is out.

"Charlie, it's a boy! We have a son! Born at one minute passed twelve, February 11," Everett exclaimed when the baby is out. Charlie is overtaken with relief that the baby is out.

"Does he have ten toes and fingers?"

Everett answered Charlie, still out of sight. "Yes, all toes and fingers are accounted for."

Charlie laid back on the bed to relax her completely spent mind and body. She closed her eyes to take a second before the placenta needed to be expelled. Pain started again, certainly not as intense so Charlie sat up ready to push that out, but when she sat up the whole room started vibrating. The walls, the bed, her body. "Oh, no, not this again!" Charlie screamed, "Everett it is happening again!" This feeling of doom shrouded her mind like a veil. "Everett, Everett, where are you?"

Charlie's whole body was paralyzed. Her eyes were shut and she couldn't open them. The vibrations become more consuming than last time this happened, Charlie could almost hear the vibrations. Like a current running through wires.

After what felt like minutes, Charlie could feel her body freeing up and the sensations passing. Becoming less extreme. Charlie is tired and her eyelids were heavy but she could move them. It took some effort and a minute, but she slowly worked her way from a twitch to lifting them.

The light is so bright Charlie struggled to adjust. "Everett, turn the lights off, it is hurting my eyes." Charlie's body did not respond to the brain's message to lift her hand to shield her eyes. Charlie felt very groggy and heavy.

Charlie heard a woman's voice calling for a doctor to come, saying something about the patient being awake, but Charlie only registered this as background noise. "Everett, are you watching TV?" Charlie tried to move again and open her eyes fully. She wanted to reach for Everett and have him comfort her. Charlie groaned with each fiber of effort she exerted; she didn't have much left after giving birth.

Charlie found it strange that she hadn't heard the baby cry yet. Isn't that a bad sign she hadn't heard the baby make any noise? All she could hear are voices and beeping and humming. "Everett, where's the baby, is he okay?"

"Ms. Wolfe, my name is Dr. Withsmith. Can you hear me?"

The stranger's voice startled Charlie, and then someone is prying her eyes open and flashing a light directly into them.

Where was Everett and who is touching her? Where is her baby? "Where is Everett and where is my baby?" She let her inside voice outside to ask the questions.

"Ms. Wolfe, you are in a cancer treatment center. I am Dr. Withsmith. You have been in a coma for almost nine months now. Do you understand what I am saying to you?"

Confusion went on overdrive and sped away with Charlie's abilities to rationalize what she is hearing. "Where is Everett and where is my baby?" Charlie is forcing with all her will and might to start moving. Trying to get away from wherever she was and get back to her husband and life. In her mind she is thrashing around but on the outside her arms and legs were twitching slightly.

"Ms. Wolfe, there is no Everett and you don't have a baby. I know this must come to you as a bit of a shock but you were admitted ten months ago for liver cancer treatment, and nine months ago you tried to take your own life causing brain damage and you fell into a coma." Dr. Withsmith touched Charlie's hand to provide some comfort as the nurses busied around Charlie, checking on her condition.

Charlie heard the words but refused to accept them. She must be dreaming. She gathered up some courage to open her eyes fully, now that she had adjusted to the bright light, and when she opened them a man in a white lab coat stood in front of her. Behind him are medical machines beeping and flashing. The room is not her home, but it is a hospital room, cold and bare.

Charlie's mind just couldn't deal with the information, it refused to understand so it shut down. Charlie's emotional center understood on the other hand, and she began to sob uncontrollably. She cried herself to sleep, hoping she could go home now. Last thing she heard were some nurses saying how this must be hard, and who was Everett. They would check her family history to see if it was a family member.

## Chapter 40

## Alone

In the coming days Charlie finally started to accept her new reality. She went through all the stages of loss all over again for her fictious husband and child, and perfect life. She is elated to hear that her parents and brother are still alive and found comfort in their presence.

To see her mother again is soul filling; she had missed her so much, well, the feelings from in her coma. The feelings felt so real. Charlie kept feeling for the wedding ring Everett had given her, causing her heart to bleed each time it isn't there. She is filled with love for her family but life-ending grief for the loss of the life she had lived for the past nine months.

Charlie is happy to hear that half the world had not died from a virus or vaccine, but they were in a state of a pandemic. Life is as she knew it before. She didn't want that life, because that meant she still had cancer and there is no Everett. Well, the chemo treatments had worked while in a coma and she is in remission, but still no Everett.

In the subsequent weeks Charlie learnt that Everett had been a patient in the same treatment center as her, he was in the bed next to hers. They chatted a bit when she had first arrived, he had already been there. Charlie was depressed and not interested in making new friends when she was on the way out. She doesn't remember him as a body but she does remember him as a voice. She does remember the brief exchange of small talk. She knew he had skin cancer, not brain, and that he was a fire chief in Seattle and not a naval officer in the Canadian Navy.

The nurses had told Charlie that his treatments had worked, as well. He had beaten cancer. He is also the one that saved her life when Charlie had tried to commit suicide. He had checked on her a couple of times afterwards when she had fallen into a coma but hadn't been around in months. The nurse offered to call him for Charlie to see if he could come for a visit, if Charlie wanted.

Charlie had some feelings to work through and thought about that offer for another week. Charlie is afraid she would be disappointed; he wouldn't be the same or live up to his fictious self. But in the end life with Everett is worth at least trying, a fraction of what they had in her mind would fill her empty heart. Even if that meant it is only as friends. The nurse reported back to her that Everett would come to see her in a week. That is when she is due to be moved to a recovery center for the atrophy and mobility part of coming out of a coma. Charlie somehow felt better and had something to fight for. Charlie decided to start again.

This is not the end – this is only the beginning!

# About the Author

Debut author Nathalie Edwards enjoys painting, jogging, hiking and exploring the island that inspired the setting of Starting Again. As a lifelong lover of books, Nathalie has been exploring her creative side in recent years and decided to try her hand at writing one.

Although originally from Montreal, Quebec, she currently lives in Qualicum Beach, British Columbia, with her husband and son, and their two beloved dogs.

Printed in Canada